THE ITALIAN'S
PASSIONATE
REVENGE

THE ITALIAN'S PASSIONATE REVENGE

BY

LUCY GORDON

MILLS & BOON®

Pure reading pleasure™

First published in Great Britain 2008
Large Print edition 2008
Harlequin Mills & Boon Limited,
Eton House, 18-24 Paradise Road,
Richmond, Surrey TW9 1SR

ISBN: 978 0 263 20075 1

Set in Times Roman 16 on 17¾ pt.
16-0908-58396

Printed and bound in Great Britain
by Antony Rowe Ltd, Chippenham, Wiltshire

CHAPTER ONE

WHO is he? Why has this stranger come to my husband's funeral and why does he stand there, staring at me across the grave?

'Ashes to ashes, dust to dust—'

In a corner of a London cemetery the preacher intoned the words over the open grave, while the mourners shivered in the cold February drizzle and the dead man's widow wished it could all soon be over.

Ashes and dust, she brooded. A perfect description of my marriage.

Elise ventured a glance around the others and saw only blank faces, just as she'd expected. Ben Carlton had had business associates, but no friends. His life had been a litter of shady deals and shabby relationships.

Including ours, Elise thought. A wretched marriage, for wretched reasons, brought to a wretched end.

Many of the people here were unfamiliar. Some she'd met at the lavish dinner parties Ben had enjoyed giving, and she vaguely recalled their faces. Some she'd seen at functions hosted by his firm. Others she'd never seen. They all looked alike, except for one man.

He stood on the other side of the grave, his lean face expressionless, his eyes hard as they watched her. As the last rites dragged on, Elise realised that he never looked at the coffin, only at herself. He had a fixed gaze, with something unyielding about it, as though by staring her down he could find the answer to a question.

She tried to tear her eyes away, but she couldn't. It was almost as though he was ordering her to look at him, refusing to release her. She fought him but, to her dismay, she could feel her will yielding to his.

He was in his late thirties, tall, dark-haired, with a commanding air that seemed to reduce everyone else to insignificance. He spoke briefly as he stepped aside to let a lady pass. It was only a few words, but Elise heard the Continental accent and wondered if he was attached to Farnese Internationale, the great Italian-based firm that had recently hired Ben, an act that still baffled her.

Elise hadn't known much about her late

husband's business affairs, beyond a vague suspicion that others considered him an oaf. Nothing had surprised her more than seeing him headhunted by a powerful multinational corporation.

Ben had told her about it, smirking with self-congratulation. He'd known about her poor opinion of him and had relished the chance to prove her wrong.

'You just wait until we're living in Rome, in the lap of luxury,' he crowed. 'The apartment will make your eyes water.'

That was how she discovered that he'd already bought the apartment, without consulting her. Worse, he'd even sold their London home, behind her back.

'I don't want to go back to Rome,' she told him furiously. 'And I'm amazed that you do. Do you think I can forget—?'

'Don't talk rubbish. That business was over long ago. I've got an important job and we'll have to do a lot of entertaining. You should be looking forward to it. It'll give you a chance to use your Italian again. You always spoke it well.'

'You said yourself, that was a long time ago,' she reminded him.

'Look, I'm going to need you,' he said in the brusque way he always used to end arguments. 'I don't speak the damned language and you do, so don't give me a hard time.'

'Plus you got one jump ahead by getting our money out of the country before I found out.'

He looked pleased.

'Just in case you were getting any ideas about divorce—' he chuckled '—I know what's been flitting through your head.'

'Perhaps I'll decide to go my own way and earn my own living,' she mused.

How that had made him hoot with laughter!

'You? After all these years of living the good life? Never! You've gone soft.'

Elise had ignored his rudeness and selfish complacency, being used to it. Perhaps he was right and she could no longer function independently. It was a dispiriting thought.

With their house sold, they'd moved into The Ritz Hotel until the day of departure. But that day had never come. Ben had died of a heart attack while enjoying an assignation in another hotel with a woman who'd called an ambulance, then vanished before it could arrive.

Elise shivered. It was late afternoon and the light had faded, turning the mourners into shadows. Still she sensed the stranger watching her in the gloom.

At last it was over and people began to move, reminding her to perform her duties as hostess.

'I do hope you can come to the reception,' she said again and again. 'It would have meant so much to Ben.'

'I trust your invitation includes me,' said the man. 'You don't know me, but I'd been looking forward to your husband joining my firm. My name is Vincente Farnese.'

She knew the name at once. She'd heard it often from Ben's lips—one of the most powerful men in Italy—had the ear of government ministers—influential—rich—

'And he wants me to join him,' Ben had rejoiced. 'He searched for me, said only the right man would do for the position—offered me a fortune—said it was worth anything to get me—'

Elise had smothered her astonishment that anyone should actually seek out this overblown windbag, never mind pay him over the odds. Now she stared at Vincente Farnese, searching for some clue to help solve the mystery.

She found none. He was in the prime of life, with the air of a man of sense. It was inexplicable.

'I've heard of you from my husband,' she said. 'It was good of you to take the trouble to attend his funeral. Of course you're welcome at the reception.'

'You're too kind,' he said smoothly.

A man who was never at a loss, she thought, ready with the right words, the right attitude, always ahead.

So why had he bothered to come here? What could he hope to gain now Ben was dead?

Suddenly she didn't care any more, about anything. There was only a weary longing for all this to be over. She closed her eyes, swaying slightly, then felt strong hands steadying her.

'Not much longer,' said Vincente's quiet voice.

The words echoed her thoughts so exactly that she opened her eyes sharply and found him standing close, holding her gently.

'Don't give up now,' he murmured.

'I wasn't—that is—'

'I know,' he said, and she had the strangest feeling that he did.

He began to guide her towards the car, waving away the chauffeur to open the door for her himself. Just before she got in, Elise glanced up at someone else who'd caught her eye in the cemetery. This was a woman in her thirties, attractive in a flashy way, wearing expensive black clothes that somehow managed to look blowsily overdone.

It occurred to Elise that this stranger too had been regarding her oddly, with a kind of belligerence, hating her and sizing her up at the same time. But Signor Farnese had occupied her thoughts, leaving her little attention to spare.

'Who is that lady?' he asked, getting in beside Elise.

'I don't know. I've never seen her before.'

'She seems to know you, if the looks she's been giving you are anything to go by.'

It was a short journey to The Ritz, where a lavish buffet had been laid on in the grandiose suite Ben had insisted on occupying. Elise would have preferred a quiet affair, but she'd splashed out on Ben's funeral out of a kind of guilt. Now he was dead she felt uneasy about her hostility, no matter how much he'd deserved it. She couldn't grieve but she could give him the kind of send-off he would have wanted, suitable for a wealthy, important man, even if the wealth had often been a conjuring trick and the importance had existed only in his head.

As she entered the room a mirror told her that she looked perfect for the role of elegant widow in her neatly fitting black dress, small black hat over blonde hair, styled severely. She was an expert in the art of appearance, having once dreamed of being a clothes designer. Events had ended her training abruptly, but her skill remained.

Without conceit, Elsie knew that she was beautiful. For the last eight years she'd had nothing to do except be lovely, elegant and sexy, because that was what Ben had wanted. She had been his property and he'd expected his property to be perfect. Her life had become a round of gym sessions and beauty parlours.

Nature had given her the good looks to start with, a figure that was easy to keep slim, hair that was naturally blonde and luxuriant, eyes that were large and deep blue. The arts of the coiffeur and masseuse had been employed to great effect, until she'd turned into the perfect finished article.

She was everything the world expected—graceful, chic, always uttering the right words. Only she knew how empty she was inside. But she did not care.

There was another truth about her, but she'd lost sight of it so long ago that she'd almost forgotten it. In that hidden place there was wild feeling, death-defying emotion, passionate desire. She'd shut those away when she'd married Ben and now she could no longer find the key.

Elise made her rounds, ensuring that everyone had enough to eat and drink and the proper attention. But proper for what? She no longer had any connection with these people. Soon she would be completely free.

Just a little longer, she promised herself.

Signor Farnese was occupying himself talking with the other guests.

Networking, she thought, remembering Ben at similar gatherings.

But this was different. Ben had always been trying to attract the attention of the others, seeking to impress them. With Vincente Farnese it was the opposite. Everyone knew who he was and wanted to catch his eye. If it pleased him he acknowledged their presence, otherwise he dismissed them with a brief nod, courteous but final.

He was everything that Ben had wanted to be, she thought—a handsome, healthy animal, with a face that, despite its strength and good looks, was also shrewd and wary, giving him an edge of danger. His eyes were the darkest she had ever seen, yet an all-seeing light came from their depths. He looked as if he'd mastered life, and intended to go on mastering it.

The chief lion in the pack, she thought. So why is he here?

He was abstemious—eating nothing and making one glass of wine last for two hours—and, to her heightened imagination, there seemed something ominous even in that.

The woman Elise had noticed ate and drank

with gusto. Like the man, she seemed to be waiting for something.

At last the goodbyes were said and Elise turned with a fixed smile to address her unknown guest.

'I'm so sorry, we haven't been introduced,' she said politely. 'It was so kind of you to—'

'Don't waste time with that stuff,' the woman interrupted rudely. 'Don't you know who I am?'

'I'm afraid I don't. Were you a friend of my husband?'

'Friend? Hah! You could put it like that.'

'I see.'

'And what's that supposed to mean?'

'Perhaps you were with him when he had his heart attack?'

The woman gave a squeal of laughter, full of wine.

'No, I heard about that, but it wasn't me. I must say I've got to hand it to you, cool as a cucumber in front of all these people, when you must have known what everyone was thinking.'

'What matters is that none of them knew what *I* was thinking,' Elise said.

'Oh, good for you! You're diamond-hard, aren't you?'

'When I have to be,' Elise said quietly. 'Perhaps you should be careful.'

The waiters were clearing away. Elise stood back to let them depart, then returned to what was clearly going to be a battle. Fine. She was just in the mood.

'Who are you?' she demanded.

'Mary Connish-Fontain,' said the other woman deliberately, stressing the double barrel.

'Is that supposed to mean something to me?'

'It will, when I'm finished. I came here to demand justice for my son. *Ben's* son!'

Out of the corner of her eye Elise was aware that Vincente Farnese had become mysteriously alert, although he never moved.

'You had a son by my husband?' Elise asked slowly.

'His name's Jerry. He's six.'

Six. Elise had been Ben's wife for eight years. But it wasn't a surprise.

'Are you saying that Ben was supporting you?' Elise asked. 'I don't believe it. I've been through his financial affairs and there's nothing about you or a child.'

'There wouldn't be. We broke up before Jerry's birth. He—he didn't want to hurt you.'

If Elise had believed her before, she didn't now. Ben had never cared about hurting her.

'I married someone else,' Mary went on. 'But now we've split up.'

'What's his name?' Signor Farnese asked suddenly.

'Alaric Connish-Fontain,' Mary said, puzzled. 'Why?'

'It's an unusual name. I recognised it at once. Your husband's crash into bankruptcy was really spectacular. No wonder you're looking for new fish to fry.'

'How dare you?' Mary snapped.

'Forgive me. Your motives are, of course, as pure as the driven snow.'

'How did he feel about Ben's son?' Elise intervened.

Mary shrugged. 'He thought Jerry was his.'

'But when he lost all his money Jerry suddenly became Ben's,' Elise said scornfully. 'Don't take me for a fool.'

'No, don't do that,' agreed Signor Farnese.

'You can say what you like,' Mary snapped. 'I want what's right for my son. He should be Ben's heir and I'm going to see that he is. You've got a posh house, so sell it, and I want half. *What are you smiling for?*'

The last words came out as a scream, for Elise had started to laugh. She shook with mirth until she felt she might choke, while her enemy regarded her in frustration.

'I'm telling you, sell your house,' she repeated furiously.

'There is no house,' Elise said, calming herself. 'That's why I'm living in a hotel. Ben already sold our house. It was his way of forcing me to go to Italy with him.'

'Then you've got the money. I know all about property laws—'

'Somehow that comes as no surprise,' the dark Italian murmured. 'If there's one woman I feel I could rely on to know about property laws, it's you.'

'So I've protected myself, so what? Husband and wife own the marital home jointly—'

'True,' Elise agreed. 'That's why Ben went about it in a twisty way. First he took out a huge mortgage on our London home, forging my signature when necessary. Then he bought a place in Italy. By the time I found out, it was too late. The money was already out of this country.'

'Don't give me that,' Mary sneered. 'You married Ben for his money and you've had eight years to put aside a nest egg for yourself.'

Sick loathing rose in Elise and for a blinding moment she nearly blurted out the truth—that she'd cared nothing for Ben's money, had married him only to head off a threat to her beloved father, who could have gone to gaol with the evidence in Ben's possession.

But she forced herself to stay silent. The years of her dreadful marriage had taught her self-control.

'There's no nest egg,' she said. 'You can believe that or not, as you like.'

'And yet you've got enough to live here.' Mary's gesture took in their luxurious surroundings.

'No, I haven't. I'm moving out to somewhere cheaper as soon as possible.'

'Wherever you go, I'll be on your tail.'

A change came over Vincente Farnese. Mary couldn't see his face clearly but Elise could, and she thought it was like seeing someone become possessed by the devil. Whatever idea had flashed across his brain made his eyes glint and a wicked smile touch his mouth.

A devil, but a humorous devil, she thought.

'I shouldn't do that if I were you,' he advised, facing Mary full on. 'She has a heart of stone and a brain of ice. She'll outwit you every time.'

'You make her sound like a cold-hearted bitch,' Mary sneered. 'I guess you know her really well.'

'You're right. I've learned exactly how ruthless she can be.'

Bemused, Elise regarded him.

A knowing look came into Mary's eyes. She'd misunderstood, as he'd meant her to.

'Got her claws into you too, has she?' she demanded coarsely. 'I know all about her. Ben told me how she chased him for his money, then did the dirty on him when they were married.'

'That's a lie!' Elise burst out. 'I never chased Ben. He came chasing after me, all the way to Rome—'

'Just as you meant him to. You knew how to make him come grovelling. As for you—' she pointed a finger at Vincente '—I'll bet your wife doesn't know you're here.'

'I have no wife,' he retorted. 'I've never been tempted into the married state and at times like this I'm deeply glad of it. Tell me, ladies, is there a woman in the world who sincerely regrets the man she's put behind her—for one reason or another?'

Mary gave a contemptuous snort. 'Had your fill of you, has she? And now she doesn't care who she hurts. I don't suppose she ever has.'

'That's true,' he said softly. 'You don't know how true that is.'

'So what are you doing here now? Think there's something here for you? Haven't you learned your lesson?'

Vincente shrugged and spoke with a sigh that Elise guessed was as false as his regretful manner.

She had to hand it to him for a magnificent if dishonest performance.

'There are some women who can affect a man like that,' he mourned. 'So that he forgets everything he knows about her and still lives in hope.'

'But I'm not a man,' Mary snapped. 'I'm not giving up until I get what's right.'

'But this isn't the way,' he said smoothly. 'Arm yourself with a DNA test and Mrs Carlton won't be able to argue.'

'Ah, but he's dead,' Mary said quickly. 'It's too late for a test.'

'The hospital where he died will have blood samples,' Elise pointed out. 'They can be tested and then we'll know for certain.'

Strangely, this prospect did not seem to ease Mary's mind.

'You don't need a test,' she said edgily. 'Jerry's Ben's son, no doubt of it. We can sort something out between us, then I'll go—'

'You'll go now if you know what's good for you,' Elise snapped. 'I wasn't born yesterday. If you're still here in ten seconds—'

'Are you threatening me?'

'Yes, that's exactly what I'm doing,' Elise flung at her in cold fury. She was possessed by the joy and satisfaction of losing her temper. It was glorious.

'You'll be hearing from my lawyer—'

'Get out!'

Whether it was something she saw in Elise's face, or whether it was Vincente urging her towards the door, Mary suddenly couldn't get out fast enough.

'I'll be back,' she threatened. 'You may think you've got away with it—'

'But she won't,' Vincente assured her. 'There's always justice in the end, however long the wait.'

He left the room with her and Elise could hear murmurs from the hall outside until he returned a few moments later.

'Are you all right?' he asked, startled by her flushed cheeks and flashing eyes.

'Everything's wonderful,' she said firmly. 'I haven't enjoyed myself so much in years. She actually thought I'd just cave in.'

'How very foolish of her,' he said, amused.

'Another minute and I'd have lost control and done something we'd both have regretted.'

'Not you. You were always in control, that was why you were impressive. Pure steel. Admirable.'

'Thank you. But don't tell me she just calmly left.'

'I've told her how to contact me,' he said. 'And gave her my best advice. She won't trouble you for long.'

'I suppose it's always possible that her son is Ben's,' Elise observed, not sounding greatly interested.

'No. Last year her husband was featured in a magazine—great financier, devoted family man, et cetera. There was a picture of him and his son, with a strong likeness between them. She was trying it on with you because she needs money. Forget her.'

Elise gave a soft choke of laughter. 'You made her think you're going to help her.'

'It was the simplest way to get rid of her. Or are you so shocked at my methods that you won't accept my help?'

'No—oh, no—'

The laughter was welling up in her now, uncontrollable. She'd endured the strains and tensions of the day, but having them suddenly removed was a shock that left her unsteady.

'*Signora—?*' His voice was gentle but he raised it when she didn't seem to hear him. '*Signora!*'

She managed to shut off the sound but her whole body still shook, though whether it was laughter or trembling he was no longer sure.

'I'm all right—really,' she managed to say.

'You're not. You're far from all right. Come here.'

He spoke brusquely and jerked her suddenly

against him, holding her, not tenderly but firmly like iron, so that her flesh received a message of safety that infused her whole self, reaching her heart, making her relax.

It was crazy, Elise thought. She didn't know him but his grip had the power to steady her.

She ought to push him away, not stand tamely in his arms. But the strangest feeling was creeping over her, as though here and only here was comfort and all would be well while he held her.

When she spoke she could hear her voice shaking.

'I'll be all right when I've calmed down. Perhaps you should go now.'

'No, I won't leave you like this. You shouldn't be alone. Sit down.'

He guided her to a chair and left her for a moment, returning with a glass which he held out.

'Drink this.'

Another choke of laughter burst from her. 'It's champagne.'

'It's all I could find. They seem to have cleared everything else away.'

'I can't drink champagne at my husband's funeral.'

'Why not? You didn't give a damn for him, did you?'

She looked up and found him watching her with an inscrutable expression.

'No,' she said after a moment. 'I didn't.'

Elise took the glass, drained it and held it out for a refill.

He obliged and watched her drink the second glass before saying, 'Then I wonder why you've been crying so much.'

'What do you mean? You haven't seen me shed a tear today.'

'Not today, no. But when you're alone.'

It was true. In the depths of the night she'd wept her heart out, not for Ben, but for her desolate life, her ruined hopes, above all for the laughing young man who'd come and gone so many years ago. There was nothing of him now but aching memories.

It could all have been so different. If only—

Desperately she shut that idea off, as she'd done so often before.

But how had this man known?

'It's in your face,' he said, answering her unspoken question. 'You tried hard to conceal the truth, but make-up can only do so much.'

'It fooled the others.'

'But not me,' he said softly.

At any other time she might have thought she heard a warning. Now there was only relief that he seemed to understand so much.

'Drink up,' Vincente said suddenly, 'and I'll take you out for a meal.'

His lordly assurance that she would follow his lead irritated her.

'Thank you, but I'd rather stay here.'

'No, you wouldn't. You don't want to be on your own in this empty place that's much too big for you.'

'Ben insisted on a huge suite,' she said instinctively.

'So I'd have expected. He had to show off, didn't he?'

'Yes, but—I won't discuss him with you. He's dead. Let that be an end.'

'But death is never really the end,' he pointed out. 'Not for those left behind. Don't stay here alone. Come out with me and say all the things you couldn't say to anyone else. You'll feel better for it.'

Suddenly she longed to do as he suggested. After today she need never see him again, and in that was a kind of freedom.

'All right,' she said. 'Why not? Yes, I'll come,' she repeated, as though trying to convince herself.

'You'd better change out of that black first.'

She'd been going to do just that, but again his cool way of dictating to her made her rebellious.

'Don't give me orders.'

'I'm not. I'm only suggesting what you want to

do anyway,' he said, assuming a reasonable air that was almost as amusing as it was annoying.

It was an act. Nothing about this man was reasonable.

'Indeed? And have you any "suggestions" for what I should wear?'

'Something outrageous.'

'I don't do "outrageous".'

'You should. A woman with your face and figure can be as outrageous as she likes, and it's her duty to make use of her gifts. Because I'm sure Ben would have preferred that. I'll bet money that somewhere in your wardrobe there's a "flaunt" dress that he wanted people to see you in, with him,' Vincente said with confidence.

'But Ben isn't here. And if I go out with you people will say, "She's wearing *that* when she's just buried him?"'

'So let them call you scandalous. What do you care?'

'I ought to care,' she said, trying to conceal how shockingly tempting was the picture.

'But you *don't*. Perhaps you never did. This is no time to start.'

'You've got it all worked out.'

'I always plan ahead. It's a great help in covering every angle.'

'You should be careful, covering too many angles. It looks suspicious,' Elise replied.

That checked him, she was glad to notice, and made him regard her uncertainly.

'What do you mean by that?' he asked.

'In another age they'd have called you a wizard and burnt you at the stake.'

'Whereas now they call me a wizard and buy my shares. No more talking. Time to be outrageous. Hurry. Don't keep me waiting.'

Elise went into the bedroom, thinking that it was simply indecent that he should have known about her 'flaunt' dress.

It hung in the far corner of her wardrobe, low-cut, whispering honey-coloured silk that sparkled with every movement. Ben had chosen it.

'You can wear it to do me proud,' he'd declared.

'I'd wear it if I wanted to be taken for a certain kind of woman,' she'd protested.

'Nonsense! If you've got it, flaunt it.'

He'd actually said that.

She'd worn it once and felt self-conscious at the way it hugged her so tightly that it was impossible to wear anything underneath, and emphasised every movement of her hips.

It was cut on the slant, clinging lovingly to her, the neckline so low as to be barely decent, the extra length at the back making a slight train. It was impossible to walk normally in such a dress. Only sashaying would do.

Elise tried it, watching her own provocative movements before the mirror, and was shocked at herself for enjoying it. But tonight she was a different person.

Taking a deep breath, she flung open the door and walked out.

The room was empty.

CHAPTER TWO

LOOKING round in strong indignation, Elise realised that Vincente Farnese had made a fool of her—teasing her expectations, then leaving her stranded. But the next moment there was a knock on the door and she opened it to find him there.

'I went upstairs to my own room to change for the evening,' he explained.

'You're staying here?'

'Certainly. I don't have a base in London. This seemed the best idea. May I say that you look magnificent? Each man there will envy me.'

'Don't talk like that,' she said sharply.

'Why not? Isn't it what every woman likes to hear?'

'I'm not every woman. I'm me. Ben used to say things like that, as though all that mattered was how he seemed to other people. It was horrible, and if you're the same the whole thing's off. In fact—'

'Forgive me,' he said, interrupting her quickly. 'You're right, of course. I shall say no more about your beauty. My car is waiting.'

Vincente took the velvet wrap that she'd brought out, placing it delicately around her shoulders.

The limousine stood by the entrance, the chauffeur holding open the rear door. Elise slid gracefully into place in the back seat and he followed her.

It was a short journey to a street in Mayfair, and a door that seemed to fade unobtrusively into the wall. Set into it was a small plaque that said 'Babylon'.

Elise raised her eyebrows at one of the most exclusive nightclubs in London. Only members were admitted and membership was almost impossible to obtain. Ben's application had been refused, much to his fury.

But Vincente Farnese, despite having no base in London, was a member who received an immediate respectful greeting.

'We're a little early,' he said as they descended the long stairway, 'so we can eat in peace and talk quietly before the music starts.'

He was a skilled host, with a connoisseur's knowledge of exquisite food and wine. Elise had thought she wasn't hungry, but when she tried the miniature crab cakes with sauce *rémoulade* she discovered otherwise.

For a few minutes they paid the food the tribute of silence, but she smiled and nodded in recognition of his choice. She was beginning to relax. Somehow it no longer seemed bizarre to be here on such a day, as though these hours existed in a cocoon, away from real life. Tomorrow the problems would be there, but tonight she could float free of them.

'Why did you tell that woman I had a heart of stone?' she asked. 'You know nothing about me.'

'We needed to convince her that you were formidable.' After a moment he added, 'And every woman can turn her heart to stone when she needs to. I think you've sometimes needed to.'

'True. She wasn't the only one.'

'Was he ever faithful to you?'

'I doubt it. He must have taken up with her pretty soon after our marriage.'

'Does that surprise you?'

'Nothing I discover about Ben surprises me any more.' She shrugged. 'Even the way he died.'

'I heard some strange rumours about that.'

'You mean the woman he was with when he had the heart attack? She vanished so nobody knows who she was.'

'A ship that passed in the night.'

She gave a wry smile. 'There was a whole flotilla of those.'

'That must have been very hard for you.'

'I feel sorry for him more than anything, being left alone like that. I may not have been a very good wife, but I'd have stayed with him when he was ill.'

'Weren't you a good wife?'

'No,' she said shortly. 'I wasn't.'

'Surely you must have loved him at some point?'

'I never loved him,' she said simply, wondering why she was telling so much to this man.

'That's very interesting.'

'I see. You're another who thinks I married Ben for what I took to be his vast wealth. Give me patience!'

'I don't—'

'Listen, you said yourself, I don't care what people say about me. You're right, and "people" includes you. Think what you like.'

Silence.

'I apologise,' he said quietly.

'No, I suppose *I* should apologise,' she said wryly.

'Don't spoil it. I'm impressed—almost as impressed as I was when you dealt with Mary. I made a note then not to get on your wrong side. Can't you tell that I'm shaking in my shoes?'

'Oh, stop it,' she said, laughing unwillingly.

'It's natural that your nerves should be on edge after what you've been through.'

'And *stop* being sympathetic and understanding. It doesn't suit you.'

'How shrewd of you to have spotted that!'

Another silence, until Vincente said in a voice full of relief, 'Ah, here's our main course.'

It was roast tenderloin of beef with sauce Béarnaise, served with red wine, which he poured for her.

Suddenly he spoke in Italian. 'Ben told me you'd be valuable to him in Rome. He said you'd been there and spoke Italian pretty well.'

She replied in the same language. 'I studied fashion in Rome before I married him. My Italian really isn't that good. I haven't spoken it for a while.'

'It's not bad,' he said, reverting to English. 'You'd soon become fluent again. How long were you there?'

'Three months.'

'And in that time you must have had many admirers.'

He spoke in a mischievous voice and she laughed in return.

'I had flirtations. After all, you know—Italian men…' She shrugged, keeping it light.

'I know that no true Italian man could look at you without wanting to become your lover,' he said in the same tone.

'Maybe it wasn't just what they wanted. Perhaps my own wishes came into it as well,' she said with a touch of irony.

'And you're telling me that not one young man managed to make himself agreeable to you? *Ai-ai-ai!* The men of my race are losing their touch. Not a single one?'

'I forget,' she riposted. 'There was such a crowd.'

He laughed aloud, his eyes gleaming with appreciation, and raised his wineglass in salute.

'Truly you are a cold-hearted goddess. All that youthful ardour at your feet and not one young man stands out in your mind?'

'Not one,' she lied.

'How long after returning from Rome did you marry Ben?'

'Almost at once.'

'Then the mystery is solved. You were in love with him all the time and abandoned your design course to marry him.'

'I've already told you I didn't love him.'

'Just why did you marry him?' Vincente demanded abruptly. The humour had gone from his voice.

'Why, for his money, of course,' Elise said with a shrug. 'I thought we settled that earlier.'

'Somehow that doesn't convince me. There must have been another reason.'

Suddenly the air seemed to shiver.

'Signor Farnese,' Elise said coolly, 'please stop interrogating me. None of this is your business, and I will not discuss my private affairs with you.'

'I'm sorry,' he said quickly. 'I was only making small talk.'

'Really? It was almost like being interviewed for a job.'

'Then I blame myself. I assess many people for jobs and I'm afraid it creeps into my manner in the rest of life. Forgive me.'

It was said charmingly and she let it go at that. She still sensed that there was something else going on, but it wasn't worth pursuing. After tonight she would never meet him again.

'What do you plan to do now?' he asked.

'I'm not really sure. Ben's death was so sudden, and there's been so much to do that I haven't had time to think.'

'Come back to Rome with me.'

'What for? Ben won't be working for you now.'

'But you own an apartment there.'

'An agent can sell it for me. I don't need to be there.'

'Can't you simply treat yourself to a holiday?' When she hesitated he said urgently, 'When you were there as a young girl, did you ever visit the Trevi Fountain?'

'Of course,' she murmured.

Elise had been to the great fountain in the company of a young man with a bright face and a merry laugh.

'You must toss a coin in and make a wish,' he told her.

She'd taken out a coin, musing, 'What shall I wish for?'

'There's only one wish—that you will return to Rome.'

'All right.' She tossed her coin into the water and cried aloud to the sky, 'Bring me back.'

'Come back for ever,' he urged.

'For ever and ever!' she cried ecstatically.

'Never leave me, *carissima*.'

'Never in life,' she vowed.

'Love me always.'

'Until my last moment.'

A month later she'd left Rome, had left the young man, had never seen either of them again.

'And like all visitors you tossed a coin in and wished to return to Rome?' Vincente said now. 'It is now the time to make that wish come true. Come with me and see if it's still the city of your memories.'

She shook her head. 'Memories are never the same. You can't go back.'

'Are the memories so terrible that you're afraid to confront them?'

'Perhaps they are.'

'Maybe the truth will be better than your fears?'

She shook her head. 'That never happens,' she said with soft violence. *'Never!'*

'So you've discovered that, have you?' he asked sombrely.

'Doesn't everyone, sooner or later?'

'Yes,' he said. 'I suppose you're right.'

The heaviness in his voice made her look up quickly and for a moment she caught an unguarded expression in his eyes. It vanished at once, but it showed her something he was trying to keep hidden. Her interest grew.

'Why are you here?' she murmured.

'I came to a funeral.'

'But why? You're here for a purpose.'

'To pay my respects.'

'I don't believe you. I don't think you "do" sweetness and light. You wouldn't head that corporation if you did.'

'Even in business some of us manage to behave like civilized human beings,' Vincente observed with a slight edge to his voice.

'But why?' she asked, apparently wide-eyed with wonder. 'There's no money in it.'

'There can be,' he said incautiously and was startled by the glint of mischief in her eyes.

'Now there's an admission!' she said with wicked delight.

'No admission at all. We've already agreed that I don't "do" sweetness and light; we should add— unless it suits me.'

'One should always add that,' she agreed solemnly.

'You think you've got me sussed,' he asked, amused.

'You and all men. I go by a simple rule. Just think the worst. I'm never wrong.'

'You might be wrong about me,' he suggested.

Elise leaned back in her chair and considered him. The lights in the clubs were low, constantly changing from green to blue to red. By chance it was red that bathed him now, giving him the look of a handsome devil.

Elise shook her head. 'No, I'm not wrong. What brought you here? Revenge?'

It was a word she ventured to choose and it made him eye her sharply.

'What did you say?'

'Revenge. Did Ben put one over on you in a deal? Was that why you wanted him in Rome?'

'Him?' Vincente gave a bark of harsh laughter. 'He never put one over on anyone. The man was a fool. Didn't you know that?'

'I'm surprised you knew it since you hired him. What use could a fool be to you? This gets curiouser and curiouser.'

'Not at all.' He gave a sardonic grin. 'For "fool" read "donkey". I can always find a use for a donkey.'

'There must be plenty of donkeys in Rome. Why Ben?'

The sound of music gave him an excuse not to answer. The musicians were in place, a young woman glided on to the stage and began to sing in a soft, throaty voice. Suddenly the floor was alive with gently swaying dancers.

'Haven't we talked enough?' he asked.

Elise nodded and dismissed the argument, which didn't really interest her anyway. She took the hand he held out to her, letting him lead her on to the floor. It would have been wiser to stay in her seat, but she was beyond wisdom. She wanted to dance with him because she wanted to be held by him, held against him. That was the plain truth.

And tonight she was going to please herself for the first time in years.

She braced herself for the feel of his hand in the small of her back, but it was still a shock through the thin material. He drew her close so that she could feel his body, his legs moving powerfully against hers, and there was no protection against that.

Had she been crazy to agree to this? Four years ago she'd thrown Ben out of her bed, and even before that her body had slept. She'd thought it was the sleep of the dead, forgetting that the dead could awaken. Now every part of her was becoming alive and the pleasure was almost painful.

She resisted it, knowing that this was one man she had to confront on equal terms. But she also sensed that she had the power to catch him off guard, which could be the best way to face him down.

The singer was crooning smoochy words of passion and pleasure.

'Remembering—all the things we've done together—wanting you—wanting everything—'

She felt his arm tighten, silently insisting that she look up, and when she did so she found his mouth so dangerously close that for a moment they were exchanging breath. The hot whisper across her lips strained her control so that she almost reached up and kissed him.

In the event, he made the first move. Or did he? His lips brushed hers so lightly that she couldn't be sure what was dream and what was reality.

Wanting everything. It was almost indecent to want everything with this stranger, but it was happening, despite her denials. His mouth was on hers, pressing lightly, then more urgently. She closed her eyes, yielding to the pure sensation, wanting more and more of it, shutting out the world.

His hand moved slowly—upwards to caress the bare skin of her back, sideways to feel the flare of her hips, lower to enjoy the soft swell of her behind moving in the dance.

For too long she'd lived like a nun, knowing there was no place in her life for desire. But now it came dancing out of the darkness, dazzling and overwhelming her with the lure of the strange and almost unknown. Inside, she was aching to be returned to life after the long sleep that had been more like a coma.

Why now? she wondered. With him?

Because he was made for seduction, her senses replied. His body was designed for sex—long, lean, hard, pared down, subtly powerful. With every touch it whispered what it could do for her, what they could do together. His movements blended with hers so that they seemed to be making love right there on the dance floor.

'What are you doing?' she whispered.

'Surely you mean what are *we* doing?' Vincente murmured almost against her lips. 'There's no mystery about it.'

'But—no—we ought to stop this now.'

'Are you sure that's what you want?' He spoke softly and his warm breath whispered against her face.

'Yes…yes, it's…what I want.'

She was lying and they both knew it. She didn't want him to stop. She wanted *him*.

Elise didn't even like Vincente Farnese particularly. What little she knew of his mind stimulated her and they had formed an alliance of convenience, but she'd also sensed a watchfulness in him, a carefully preserved distance that precluded any warmth. There was no tenderness, no meeting of the emotions.

Despite this, or perhaps because of it, she felt a desire that was liberated from all feelings—raw, basic, uncomplicated. She ached to be in his arms, in his bed. She wanted to undress before his hungry gaze, making a delicious performance of it. But she also wanted him to remove her clothes slowly—so slowly—heightening her excitement with every leisurely movement.

She longed to join her nakedness to his, feeling his fingers explore her gently, then urgently, with passionate desire ever mounting until at last his control was destroyed and he claimed her with fierce abandon.

Yes, she thought with sudden understanding, that was what she wanted most: to see this man, so sure of himself and his powers of command, lose all control because of her. That would be satisfying as nothing else would be.

Everything was there in her head, tingling along her nerves, the anticipation of what he would do and what she would do. She tried to shut off the thought, fearful lest he sense it. But, of course, he'd already sensed it. That was what made him dangerous.

'Why deny us what we both want?' he asked, reading her thoughts again in the way he did with such terrifying ease.

'I don't always take what I want,' she said slowly.

'That's a mistake. You haven't had enough pleasure and satisfaction in your life. You should take it now that you're free.'

'Free,' she echoed longingly. 'Will I ever be free?'

'What should stop you?'

'So much…so much…'

He drew her closer and laid his lips against the tender skin of her neck.

'Take what you want,' he whispered. 'Take it, pay the price, but don't waste time on regrets.'

'Is that how you live?'

'Always,' he said, turning to guide her off the dance floor. 'Let's go.'

On the journey they didn't speak, but sat together in the back of the car, watching the light and darkness flicker over each other's faces.

Conscious of eyes upon them, they walked sedately through the hotel lobby and up to her suite. Only when the door had closed behind them did he toss aside the velvet wrap and take her into his arms, raining kisses all over her neck and shoulders.

Elise threw back her head, yielding herself up to the sweet sensation, welcoming it. Each touch of his lips sparked off tremors that flowed down over her skin, between her breasts, creating life where there had been only desolation before. A deep, shuddering breath escaped her and she reached for him.

She didn't know how they got into the bedroom, but she was lying down and he was beside her, casting his jacket aside, then reaching for her dress, pulling it down to uncover her breasts.

For a moment his face, suffused with passion,

loomed over her. She reached up, meaning to pull him down to her, but her hand seemed to have a will of its own. Instead of drawing him closer, it tensed to fend him off.

'Wait,' she whispered.

He became still, frowning as though not sure he'd heard her properly.

'Wait,' she repeated. 'What's happening to me?'

It was the worst possible moment for an attack of common sense, but it had leapt on her without warning, freezing her blood, filling her with dismay at herself.

'I can't tell you that,' Vincente said. 'Only you know what you really want. If you've changed your mind, you have only to tell me to leave.'

He was breathing harshly, but he was in command of himself.

'I'm not sure—not any more. Please let me go.'

For the briefest moment he was disconcerted, but then his eyes gleamed with respect.

'Very clever—very subtle.'

'No, you're wrong. I'm not playing tricks. It's just that—' She sat up and moved away from him. 'Good grief! Today was my husband's funeral.'

'Suddenly you remember that?'

'I guess I'm more conventional than I thought I was. I'm sorry. I just can't do this.'

He too got up, retrieving his jacket from the floor.

'You may be right,' he observed. 'It will keep until we meet again.'

'I doubt that we'll ever meet again.'

In the darkness she couldn't see his face well or read its expression, couldn't see the bafflement, admiration and sheer blazing hatred that chased each other in swift succession through his eyes.

'You're wrong,' he said softly. 'This isn't the end between us. There'll come a day when you'll remember what I told you—take what you want. And then you'll take it because, in that, we're the same.'

Now her thwarted passion was punishing her, making her tremble with the violence she'd done to herself. But from somewhere she found the strength to give him a challenging look and say, 'You left something out. I'll take it when I'm ready, and not before.'

'Then there's nothing more for me to say. I will bid you goodnight.'

Before her astonished eyes, he walked calmly out of the room without a backward glance.

Vincente was just closing his suitcase the next morning when his cellphone shrilled.

'Yes?'

'It's your driver. You said to let you know if I saw her. She's just got into a taxi. I heard her tell the driver to go to the cemetery.'

'I'll be right there. Have the engine running.'

He was downstairs in a moment. As they found their way through the streets, he asked tensely, 'Are you sure you heard her correctly?'

'She definitely said St Agnes Cemetery, where she buried her husband yesterday. It's natural enough if she's grieving for him.'

Vincente didn't answer this. His eyes were fixed on the road.

By good luck he saw Elise as soon as he reached the cemetery. She'd left her taxi and was walking away. A twist in the path gave him a sideways glimpse of her, revealing that she was carrying a bouquet of glowing red roses.

Red roses. The symbol of love. It defied belief that she was putting them on her husband's grave.

He followed, taking care to remain among the trees that would hide him, and managed to get close enough to see her drop to one knee before a modest grave, contrasting with the swaggering mausoleums that littered the place. She was facing him and he could see her face well enough to detect its look of unutterable sadness as she spoke to some unseen presence.

He'd come to England seeking her, hating her, determined to make her pay for a long ago act of cruelty. He'd so nearly secured her through her husband, but the greedy fool had died and Vincente had to think of a new plan, fast.

He'd been so sure of the kind of woman he would find, but she had been different—softer, more vulnerable, more honest. But he quickly reminded himself that this was bound to be an act. She'd had years to practise it by now.

By sheer force of will he managed to keep his hatred alive.

Her passion was harder to explain away. He was no stranger to feigned desire. Attracted by his wealth, women had always put themselves out to seduce him, and everything in Elise's past warned him that she was one of that kind. But she'd turned out to be different. He'd felt her trembling in his arms and his deepest instincts had told him that she wasn't feigning. At almost any moment he could have stripped her naked and taken her with her full-hearted consent.

Until the end, when she'd fended him off with real intent, filling him with astonishment. For a moment he'd been on the verge of losing control, but he'd forced himself to calm down and leave her. He'd spent the rest of the night racked with unsatisfied desire and anger. But there had also been the dawning of respect, and that disconcerted him more than anything.

Vincente stayed hidden as she rose to go, and only came out from among the trees when she was out of sight. Then he crossed quickly to where she had been and studied the graves. He spotted the red roses at once and dropped down on one knee to read the inscription.

'George Farnaby,' he read. He had died two months ago, in December, aged sixty-four.

Frowning, Vincente reached into his pocket and drew out a small notebook. Flipping through the pages, he came to the entry he was looking for.

One final note. Her father died just before Christmas. Ben Carlton's extensive entertaining was unaffected. A guest at one of his parties says she went through the motions of being a good hostess, but looked terrible.

Vincente looked at the roses that lay, fresh and blooming, against the hard stone. At last he went away.

Elise had slept badly and awoken early. In the shower she'd turned the water down cold, trying to refresh herself enough to view her life clearly, but the world was still a confused place.

After a light breakfast she slipped out and took a taxi to the cemetery, but not to go to Ben's grave. He was already in the past, but the man who'd died two months earlier still seemed with her. As she laid her flowers on the grave she looked sadly at the headstone.

'Dad,' she whispered, 'why did you have to die now? I put up with Ben for eight years, to stop you going to gaol. "Just a little fiddle", you said. Only Ben got his hands on the evidence and he made it look not so little.

'I should have left him when you died, but I was stunned. I needed time to make plans, and then everything caught up with me. Now he's dead, I'm free, and you'd have been free too. But it's too late. Oh, Dad, I miss you so much.'

She stayed a few minutes before walking away and getting a taxi back to the hotel. A plan was forming in her mind. First she would leave the extravagant suite Ben had insisted on hiring and move into a smaller, cheaper room for a week, while she finished tying up loose ends. Then she would find a less expensive place to live while she waited for the Rome apartment to be sold.

But first she must talk to Vincente Farnese and

make it clear that what had happened between them the night before had been an aberration. After that, she would refuse to see him again, no matter how long he remained in England. It would be hard to make him understand that because he knew now that he could bring her under his spell, at least for a while. But she was resolved to be firm against all the persuasions he could muster.

Upstairs in her suite, she chose with care the words she would say to him, then stretched out her hand to the phone. But, before she could make the call, there was a knock at the door. Outside stood one of the hotel bellboys, holding out an envelope.

'This was left for you, Mrs Carlton.'

Tearing it open, she found a page scrawled in a confident, masculine hand.

I fear urgent business calls me back to Rome with no time to say goodbye to you. Forgive me this discourtesy.
I wish you well for the future.
Vincente Farnese

There was silence, broken only by the sound of a piece of paper being torn to shreds.

CHAPTER THREE

FINDING a small hotel was easy enough and suited her mood. Elise was content to slip out of sight, unnoticed by any of the people she'd associated with during her marriage. They were acquaintances, not friends.

She found a job in a shop. By day she sold flowers, in the evening she walked without worrying much where she was going. It was good to be alone. She'd been so long without peace.

At the same time she was in limbo, unable to move in any direction until the Rome apartment was sold. But that should have happened before now.

'The Via Vittorio Veneto is the heart of luxury in Rome,' the agent had told her. 'Anything there gets snapped up.'

But he'd been wrong. Three months had passed and for some reason there were still no takers.

'I've had plenty of people to see it,' he'd said, puzzled. 'They say they like it, then back off. One man definitely wanted it. I tried to call to tell you but I couldn't reach you and, by the time I could, he'd withdrawn his offer.'

'I just don't understand this.'

'Perhaps you should come over here and move in for a while. If the place looked warm and lived in, people might like it more.'

'I'll think about it,' she said. 'But I'm sure it'll sell soon.'

But it hadn't, and the day she must return to Rome was growing closer. Elise flinched from the thought. She didn't want to see that beautiful city again, with its memories of Angelo that would be everywhere—haunting her, torturing her with what might have been.

She'd told Vincente that she'd been there as a fashion student but she'd left out everything that mattered, especially the wild beauty of her love for Angelo Caroni.

She could have studied in England but she'd fled abroad to get away from the overbearing Ben Carlton and for a short glorious time she thought she'd escaped him.

Angelo had been as young and passionate as herself. They'd been like two kids, revelling in their first experience of love, giving each other silly nicknames. She was Peri and he was Derry. He'd lived in two rooms in Trastevere, the colourful, least expensive part of town. She'd moved in with him so that they could be together, away from the world.

Then Benjamin had arrived at her college, with the evidence that could have sent her beloved father to gaol. In a frantic phone call to her father she'd begged him to deny it, but he'd tearfully admitted that it was true.

At the sound of his weeping her own tears had dried. One of them had to be strong.

When she'd told Angelo that it was over there was a violent quarrel, for he was hot-blooded. He'd stormed out and for two days she hadn't seen him. Then a hand on the door had made her heart leap. But it had been Ben, who'd tracked her down in Trastevere, had come to claim her, tired of waiting.

Even then, she realised, he hadn't guessed how much he disgusted her. He'd acted like the hero of a bad movie, dragging her to the window and covering her with kisses for the world to see.

But the one who'd seen was Angelo, returning to plead with her, watching in horror as he'd looked up at the window from the garden below.

Ben had been exultant, yelling down at him, 'She's made her choice. Look!'

As long as she lived she would remember the

scream Angelo had uttered before running away into the darkness. That was the last time she had ever seen him, as Ben had hustled her away and back to England that same night.

She knew that to the world it would look as if she was abandoning a charming young lover for an older man who could give her a wealthier life-style. She cared nothing for the world's opinion, but Angelo's condemnation broke her heart.

Her marriage had followed quickly. In the dev-astation of her honeymoon she had written a long impassioned letter to Angelo, telling him that she would always love him, giving him the number of her new cellphone, praying for him to call when she was alone.

He never did. After two weeks she'd called his cellphone. But it wasn't Angelo who had answered. From the other end of the line came the tearful, desperate voice of a woman, screeching, *'Angelo e morte—morte...'*

Then she'd shut off the phone.

Angelo was dead.

Frantically Elise had tried to call back, to find out how and when he'd died, but she'd got the engaged signal, again and again.

With Ben's jealous eyes on her, there had been no chance to discover more. Angelo had been dead for years now and still she did not know how it had happened, or why. But her fears were terrible and after Ben's death they had been partly confirmed. Going through his possessions, she'd been horrified to discover the letter she had written long ago. Somehow he had contrived to steal it. Angelo had died without ever reading her passionately contrite words.

When she'd realised that her heart had broken all over again. Feelings that had slept for years had awoken to vivid, painful life. She had loved him as only the very young know how to love, and she knew it had been the same with him.

Gone for ever. For him there had been death, for her the inner death of a frozen heart.

Now Elise seemed to have no energy to do anything but wait while her life was on hold. Going to Rome might have seemed sensible, but she couldn't make herself do it. The apartment would sell, her last tie with that brilliant, painful city would be cut, and both Angelo Caroni and Vincente Farnese would be out of her life.

Not that Vincente had ever been in her life.

She had made a brief foray on to the Internet to learn something about his background.

Farnese Internationale was a conglomerate of many firms, with branches in several countries, but all sheltering under one umbrella in the Viale Dei Parioli in Rome.

At the centre of this web of power sat Vincente Farnese, who owned the largest single block of shares and had controlling power over so many others that he was almost impossible to challenge.

He was the grandson of a man who had started from nothing and built a financial empire from pure genius.

There were pictures of the Palazzo Marini—dilapidated, as it had been when he'd bought it, and then later, when he'd spent another fortune restoring it to glory. Its magnificence was breathtaking and she guessed he'd enjoyed showing the world how far he'd come.

But it seemed to Elise that Vincente had paid the price, inheriting the empire while still in his twenties. Since then he'd devoted every moment to its preservation and increase, never finding the time to take a wife, although his name had been linked with many society beauties.

Another click showed her a collection of glamorous women, sometimes alone, sometimes on his arm.

She considered them, thinking that they were more interested in him than he in them. Their eyes caressed him, gloated over him. His expression was often wry, if he was looking at them at all.

Suddenly she made a sound of exasperation at herself, clicked away from the site. Why was she bothering to study him?

She closed down the computer. After a minute she returned to it and disconnected the electricity. She couldn't have said why she did that, but it made her feel better.

Then her job, once so pleasant, grew burdensome. Jane, the owner, became engaged to a young man called Ivor, an idler who planned to live off his wife. After his first meeting with Elise, he took to dropping in to the shop when he knew he would find her alone. Soon she was slapping his hands out of the way every few minutes.

'I can't help it,' he excused himself, with an attempt at charm. 'You're really stunning, you know that?'

'And I'm not available.'

'Don't give me that.' He smirked knowingly. 'Some women are available, even when they're "not available", if you know what I mean.'

She knew exactly what he meant. Ben had said much the same.

'Sexy as hell but still a lady,' he'd drooled. 'That's what gets them going.'

Elise had put up with it from him. She was damned if she was going to put up with it again.

'Out!' she said to him when he finally went too far.

'You don't mean that.'

'I mean exactly that.'

'You know your eyes sparkle when you're angry. Come here! *Ow!*'

Ivor jumped back, rubbing his face where her palm had caught it. He flinched as her arm shot out again, but this time she gripped his ear between finger and thumb, propelling him ruthlessly out of the shop and depositing him on the pavement.

'Don't come back,' she raged.

'Now, look—'

'Beat it,' said Vincente Farnese, hauling him to his feet.

Ivor took one look at him and fled. Elise stared at the man who seemed to have appeared out of nowhere.

'Good afternoon,' Vincente said.

It was unforgivable of him to take her unawares, so that the rush of pleasure caught her off guard before she could brace herself. She even found herself smiling, which made her really cross with him.

'Every time I see you,' he observed, 'you seem to be disposing of some enemy with an efficiency that makes me nervous. Last time it was that woman; this time it was—?'

'My boss's fiancé.'

'It's nearly six o'clock,' he added. 'Will you soon be finished for the day?'

'Yes, I'm just closing the shop.'

'Then let's go for a coffee.'

She fetched her coat, locked up and led him down the street, which was inexpensive and functional, rather than elegant. They found a cheap coffee house.

'Not your normal style, I'm afraid,' she said. 'Is this a chance meeting?'

'I never leave anything to chance,' he said simply. 'I got your address from the hotel, who had it for sending on your mail. I went to your home first.'

'Really!' she said wryly, trying to picture him looking at the shabby little hotel. 'What did you think of it?'

'I can't imagine what you're doing there.'

'It's all I can afford. I keep getting bills that Ben should have settled, and I have to work to pay them.'

'You need to escape.'

'So I will when I've sold the apartment.'

'How is that going?'

She eyed him cynically, her lips twitching.

'This is the man who just told me he never leaves anything to chance. It would be easy for you to find out that it's still on the market.'

'You're right. I really meant—why is it still for sale?'

She sighed. 'You tell me. Everyone says it's in a desirable location, but either people don't offer, or they do but it falls through.'

'Well, you know my advice. Come and sell it yourself. Make it look like a home.'

'That's what the agent said.'

'And he knows his business. You should heed him.'

'Maybe I should,' she said with a brief laugh. 'I'm probably out of a job.'

He grinned. 'Good. We leave tomorrow.'

'Not so fast—'

'What's to keep you here?'

Vincente's words brought the truth home to her starkly. There was nothing for her here any longer.

'All right,' she said softly. 'I'll come.'

'Excellent. Where shall we dine tonight?'

'I'm staying at home. I have loose ends to tie up. I'll be waiting for you tomorrow morning.'

He gave her a curious look.

'Will you? Or will I arrive to find that you've slipped away like a phantom?'

But it was he who'd slipped away like a phantom

last time; she nearly said so, but checked herself. That would be admitting that she minded, conceding a point, which her instincts warned her not to do. He was handsome, charming and more dangerous than ever.

'If I say I'll be there, I'll be there.'

She spoke in a cool tone that set him at a distance. She felt safer that way, especially now that she knew she was doing what he had always meant her to do. Just as everyone did.

He walked back to the hotel with her, where they were met by Elise's boss, who'd been sitting there in a fury.

'Ivor told me how you've been throwing yourself at him,' she seethed. 'What have you got to say for yourself?'

'Well, "goodbye" is a nice word,' Elise said. 'Especially if you say it to Ivor. Here's the key of the shop. But give him the boot, Jane. You can do better than Ivor. In fact, anybody can do better than Ivor.'

Jane scowled and walked out.

'Splendid!' Vincente said. 'That's the last of your old life.'

'Until I come back and start a new one,' she reminded him. 'Goodnight, I'll see you tomorrow. What about the flights?'

'I'll take care of them.'

'Well, what time is take-off?'

'Just be ready.'

Vincente was there the next morning at nine o'clock, to find the desk manned by a bored-looking lad.

'Please inform Mrs Carlton that I'm here,' Vincente said.

The lad lifted the phone, called the room and said, 'Hello, Vi. Is Mrs Carlton there….? It's a bit early for her to have left, isn't it? Oh, checked out last night. OK.'

'Where is she?' Vincente demanded sharply as the boy replaced the receiver.

'Gone. That was the cleaner, getting the place ready for the next person.'

Vincente's face was dark. 'But *where* has she gone?'

'Dunno. I've only just come on duty. She must have been in a rush to get away though, to have left so early.'

With a sense of shock, Vincente realised that the worst had happened. He'd made the foolish mistake of trusting her and she'd given him the slip. As he turned towards the door his face was very ugly.

'Ah, here you are!'

Lost in his furious thoughts, he almost didn't hear the words or see the young woman who had just come in from the street. Then the black haze cleared and he grasped her wrist.

'Where the devil have you been?' he snapped.

'I beg your pardon?'

Her outrage startled him and he let his hand fall.

'Don't ever speak to me like that again,' she said softly. 'I'm not accountable to you for my movements.'

'They said you'd checked out.'

'I did. I paid my bill last night to speed things up this morning. Today I cleared out of the room and put my bags in the downstairs cloakroom. I just slipped out for half an hour to say goodbye to someone.'

Too late it dawned on him that she was talking about her father. He wanted to ask her about him, but controlled himself. Everything must wait until he'd got her to Italy. Then, and only then, could he be sure of arranging matters to suit himself.

And she wouldn't be able to stop him. On that he was determined. He had waited too long for this to weaken now.

'I thought you'd gone,' he said harshly.

'I told you I'd be here, and I'm here. Why are you acting as though it was the end of the world?'

He forced a smile. 'If it seems that way I apologise. I have a strict sense of time.'

'Then let's stop wasting it and go,' she said lightly.

Vincente's chauffeur fetched her bags from the cloakroom and put them in the boot of the waiting car.

'Only two bags?' Vincente queried as they headed for the airport. 'I thought you'd have more.'

'You mean what about my wardrobes full of fancy clothes? I sold them for whatever I could get.'

'Money has really been as tight as that?'

'Yes, but that's not the only reason. I didn't want memories of my marriage. It's as though I'm a different person, and I like it.'

'You like living in that place?'

'It's peaceful,' she said unexpectedly.

'But doesn't poverty come a little hard on you?'

'I can pay for my air ticket,' she said defensively.

'There'll be no need for that. I have my own plane.'

Of course! She should have thought of that.

The twin turbojet aircraft was waiting for them, engines running. Inside, it was more like a luxury hotel than a plane. The seats had safety belts, but in all else they were plush armchairs, upholstered in pale grey velvet. After take-off, a steward appeared from the well-appointed kitchen, bearing champagne, and contriving to give her a curious look without being too obvious. Amused, Elise wondered how many women had been invited on to Vincente's plane, and how she compared to the others.

They clinked glasses.

'To your new life,' he said. 'And your new freedom.'

'Why do you say it like that?' she wanted to know.

'Like what?'

'Freedom—you said it strangely, as though it had another meaning.'

'But of course it does. Freedom means something different to everyone. Only you know what it means to yourself, but I think you'll find that Rome is full of many things that you'd never thought of.'

Still she thought she could catch the echo of another meaning, but when she looked at his face his smile was like a mask.

At the airport in Rome a limousine was waiting to take them into the city. As they reached the outskirts, Elise began to watch for the places she'd known so long ago. It was easy because the car passed through Trastevere, the least expensive, most colourful part of the city. Here, she and Angelo had lived together in joy. Here, he'd seen her in Ben's arms, and had died.

'What is it?' Vincente asked, looking at her with concern.

'Nothing,' she said quickly.

'You closed your eyes, as if something had hurt you.'

'Just a headache. I didn't sleep last night.' That was true.

'Not much longer until you can take possession of your new home and rest.'

Soon they were in the beautiful Via Vittorio Veneto, a wide, tree-lined avenue where the luxury apartments could sell for millions. Elise had already gulped over the price Ben had paid, but when she saw it she had to admit that the reality was worth every euro.

The rooms were large, with high ceilings and tall windows. There were three bedrooms, including a master bedroom with an eight foot wide bed and its own bathroom in addition to the main bathroom. The floors were marble, the furniture largely antique, with much inlaid wood in designs of flowers and animals. The windows were hung with velvet and satin curtains.

Everywhere she looked she saw lavishness and costly beauty. She noticed too that the curtains, carpets and marble floors were fresh and brilliant, as though recently cleaned. Nor was there a speck of dust in the place.

'The agent has maintained it beautifully,' she observed.

'I must admit that was my doing,' Vincente said. 'I sent in an army of cleaners.'

'Would it be rude of me to ask how you got the keys to my property?'

'It would certainly be ungrateful.'

She smiled. 'Of course the agent just did as you told him. Knowing you as I do, I should have assumed that.'

'Do you know me so well?' he asked lightly.

'You mean after one brief encounter months ago?'

'Sometimes that's all it takes.'

'Don't tell me you didn't size me up as well. I'm just not sure why, unless—?'

'Unless?' he asked tensely.

'I think you size up everyone you meet. There's always a part of you standing back, calculating.'

'I can't help it. It's the businessman in me.'

'Maybe.'

'Which means that *you're* still sizing *me* up.'

'Could be,' she said, looking him in the eye.

'How am I doing so far? Do I find favour?'

'Not entirely,' she said after a moment.

Elise had the feeling she'd caught him off-guard and was glad. This man wasn't used to being judged and found wanting.

'You dislike me?' he asked lightly.

'There's a lot to like but—let's just say that

I'm not entirely convinced. I think you have a secret agenda.'

'I always do,' he said quickly. 'I told you it's part of my nature.'

'But I wonder what it is with me?'

'Perhaps merely a desire to get to know you better.'

'Is that all?'

'If I said it was, would you believe me? Let's not play games. I want to know you better, for many reasons. And some of them you understand as well as I do. We're not children.'

She met his eyes and saw in them a direct attack that hadn't been there before. It both startled and excited her and she couldn't answer.

When he realised he'd silenced her he changed tack, speaking smoothly, easily, as though to put her at her ease.

'I'm not quite the calculating monster you think. I had this place cleaned because I wanted you to feel welcome here.'

'Thank you. I didn't mean to sound ungrateful. I don't know how long I'll be here, but I'll make the most of it while I am.'

'Good, then tonight you must let me entertain you.'

'Another nightclub?'

'No, we'll eat here.'

'But I don't know my way around that kitchen yet,' she protested.

'Leave everything to me.'

'You cook as well?'

'Wait and see. I'll leave you to get settled in, and be back this evening.'

When Vincente had gone she wandered slowly through the apartment, trying to believe that this was the place Ben had bought. Even for him, this grandiose, overblown residence shrieked self-delusion.

Suddenly she no longer knew exactly who she was.

She felt even more strange when she opened her cases and removed what few possessions she had left. They looked inadequate in this splendid setting.

Vincente had spoken of a new life, a new freedom, but it was hard to feel that she belonged here.

Elise yawned, remembering that she'd had no sleep the previous night. Instead she'd lain awake, wondering at the step she was about to take. She'd meant to be so resolute, but when she'd seen Vincente again she'd known in a moment that he could set her determination at nothing.

She'd slipped out in the early hours to pay one last visit to her father's grave and returned to find

Vincente there, tense and surly. She'd responded in the same vein and so their new relationship had gotten off to a craggy start.

Which might be best.

She got under the shower and stood, relishing the water splashing over her, washing away her old life and bringing her, bright and new, into whatever lay ahead.

One wall of the shower was a mirror and she used it to study herself critically. How far away now seemed the girl who'd gone to Rome and fallen passionately in love with a young Italian, then abandoned him to his death. That girl had been slightly plump, with a pretty, innocent, un-worldly face.

Now her face was slimmer and more beautiful, her eyes seeming larger by contrast, her full mouth haunted by irony. Her body too had lost weight, perhaps a little too much, or perhaps she was merely honed to perfection, slender in the waist, but with a generous bosom. Any man would say this was a woman created for love. Which was ironic, considering her loveless life.

Then she heard his voice again.

I want to know you better, for many reasons. And some of them you understand as well as I do. We're not children.

From the start there'd been a mysterious link between them. Now he'd gone to the heart of it, astonishing her with a direct attack.

You understand as well as I do.

Elise understood perfectly. He was forcing her to face the sexual attraction that had flared between them, warning her that his patience was running out and she must soon make a decision. It was high-handed, but instead of antagonising her it caused a sense of exhilaration to stream through her.

Now it made her look again at her own body, seeing it with his eyes. Would a man want that smooth creamy skin, those long legs, rounded behind and generous breasts? It was so long since she'd asked herself that question, but she knew by instinct that the answer was yes.

At least it was yes if she'd decided to make him want her. And, as she felt the sweet tremor of anticipation go through her, she knew she'd made that decision long ago.

Elise dried herself and slipped between the smooth sheets of the grandiose master bed. It was blissful to revel in such comfort, to relax and let sleep drift over her.

For hours she lay without moving, letting herself be submerged in her new life, not fighting it now.

There were battles ahead and she must summon all her strength to make sure that she was the winner.

When she awoke Vincente was sitting on the bed, watching her.

CHAPTER FOUR

STRANGELY, it wasn't entirely a surprise to find him there. Some part of her knew that he would never be far away. But she would have given anything to understand the expression in his eyes. There was wariness, and something that was almost calculation, but there was also frank desire. The combination intrigued her.

'How long have you been there?' Elise whispered.

'Only a few moments. I knocked on the front door but there was no reply, so I used the key just once more. I'll leave it here, at the side.'

'What time is it?' she asked.

'Just past seven.'

'I've slept that long?' she demanded, startled.

'I think you needed it. I didn't want to awaken you.'

She pulled the sheet up higher, vibrantly conscious that she was wearing nothing beneath it. He had only to tug at the material and her nakedness would be revealed. The thought made her skin tingle, and although she clutched the sheet she was also tempted to release it.

'Don't hide from me,' he whispered. 'There's nowhere to hide.'

'Isn't that for me to say?' she asked with a touch of rebellion.

As she spoke she tightened her hand on the sheet, but he didn't try to take it from her. He merely laid his hand on the outside and ran his fingers lightly across her breasts, then let them drift to her waist, where he paused.

He had the cunning of the devil, she realised. The sheet might as well not be there for all the protection it gave. She felt the soft caress of his fingertips back and forth across her stomach and waited for them to go down further, while her heart raced and the breath danced in her throat.

Why didn't he pull the sheet down and touch her bare skin? But then she knew that he was waiting for her to do it, signifying that she had weakened first. It was a battle of wills and she was damned if she would let him win. But how long could she hold out while her blood raced with excitement? She knew he must be able to read her face.

But then, just when she could feel her will beginning to yield, rescue came in the form of a knock on the outer door. He snatched his hand away, muttering something she couldn't catch, and walked out quickly, closing the door behind him.

For a moment Elise could do nothing but lie there, her whole body trembling, stunned by what had happened and what she had so nearly done. Suddenly she forced herself to move, scrambling out of bed and groping frantically for something to put on. Anything would do as long as she was dressed before he returned.

She found a pair of elegant black trousers and a white blouse. Then she brushed her hair vigorously and left it loose. She wasn't going to give him the satisfaction of seeing her dressed up elaborately. When she was satisfied that her appearance suggested casual indifference, she walked out.

And was taken completely by surprise.

Voices were coming from the kitchen. There she found Vincente and a young man laying out containers of food on the table. They were just finishing as Vincente signed a paper, sending the young man on his way.

'I see you're a really great cook,' she said, amused. 'All ready prepared.'

'You do me an injustice. Only the side dishes were prepared by others. The meat I shall cook myself.'

She didn't believe him, but he was as good as his word, preparing *Abbacchio alla Romana*—pieces of suckling lamb cooked until brown, then roasted in a sauce of garlic, rosemary, vinegar and anchovy. He did this himself, waving away her offer of help.

'If you want to be useful, you can lay the table,' he said.

The china was fine and hand-painted, set off by heavy cut glass and silver cutlery. When they were ready to eat he delayed a moment to say, 'I've brought you a mobile phone. You'll need it.'

'But I have one.'

'This is an Italian phone,' he said, as though that explained everything.

It was exquisite—top of the range, with every latest gadget and several numbers already inserted for her use.

'Those are my numbers at home and at work,' he indicated. 'That one is a lawyer whom I've asked to make some arrangements on your behalf. I dare say you'll feel I assumed too much in doing so, but you may find them convenient.'

'Thank you,' she said non-committally. 'And I promise not to disturb you at work. I wouldn't dare.'

'I hope you'll call me if you should need help.'

Elise accepted because it would have been

churlish not to. Besides, it really was a lovely object and she had a weakness for high-tech toys.

He served dinner with the skill of a waiter, laying every dish before her with a flourish. There was a series of wines, a different one for every dish, each one perfectly chosen.

They kept the talk light over dinner. He told her about his firm, the branches it had in many different countries. When she asked him about the Palazzo Marini he shrugged and made a wry face.

'My grandfather bought it to show how far he'd travelled from his poor beginnings. My father wore himself out trying to keep up the pace and that's why he died in early middle age. Then it was my turn. Luckily, I'm more like my grandfather.'

'You admire him?'

'He was a great man, perhaps a little too focused on work at the expense of people, but he did a lot of good for Italy.'

Vincente went to fetch more wine. When he returned she was standing by the window with the lights dimmed, looking out over Rome, which was bathed in floodlight. He filled two glasses and came to stand behind her.

'Do you recognise anywhere?' he asked, handing her a glass.

'So many places, but they all look different now.'

He moved closer and she felt his breath on the back of her neck.

'Everything is different, even in the last few months. I've often wondered if you've thought of me as I've thought of you.'

'Are you expecting me to answer that?' she asked lightly. 'Or do you already know?'

'What you really mean is, am I conceited enough to *think* I already know? No, I'm not that sure of myself. I won't know the answer until I make love to you.'

She turned slightly, glancing at him sideways.

'Don't be so certain that you'll ever make love to me.'

'But I will. I must have you in my bed, to see if it compares with the times it's happened in my dreams.'

Elise tried to answer but something had happened to her breath. She too had had dreams in which they achieved the union denied them months ago, after their first blazing few hours.

'We came so close once,' he murmured. 'Do you remember the night we were one step away from making love?'

'It wouldn't have been love-making,' she said quickly.

'True, but if I'd said "having sex" you'd have thought me a vulgarian.'

'"Sex" would have been the truth.'

'Yes, by all means, let's be truthful. Let's say that when I held you against me I had to fight the temptation to strip every last stitch off you and see if your body was as beautiful as my senses were telling me it was.

'And then, let's be really truthful and say that this is what you wanted me to wonder, which is why you were naked under that dress.'

'It was too tight for underwear, and you made me wear it.'

'And do you always do what a man tells you to do? I don't think so. You wore it knowing how it would affect me, and it did just that. It made me want you as much as you meant it to, and it lured me into being over-confident, which I think you may also have meant.'

She smiled. 'Is that what I was thinking?' she said softly.

'Let's say you were enjoying the joke at my expense. When I ran my hands over you through that silk you knew I was relishing every detail, picturing your nakedness, determined to see every beautiful inch of you before the evening was out.'

Softly he added, 'You played games with me.'

Elise took a sip from her glass and set it down, turning to face him.

'Not entirely,' she said. 'I didn't lead you on for the pleasure of rejecting you, if that's what you're saying. I was sincere, but then—' She broke off and made a helpless gesture. 'Suddenly it felt a terrible thing to do.'

'Terrible to satisfy yourself? Or was it me you didn't want to satisfy?'

'Perhaps I just didn't want to put it to the test. After so long—' She let the implication hang in the air.

'That's important,' he agreed. 'You need exactly the right man, enticing you to pleasure subtly. It would be a difficult choice.'

She was surprised into a choke of laughter. 'Are you suggesting that I'm lining up candidates?'

'You wouldn't have to. They're already in line. I saw them at Ben's funeral, watching you, wondering if they had a chance. I doubt if Ivor was an isolated case. Even the delivery man who came here tonight gave you an appreciative look, and me an envious one.'

Vincente was telling her that they had come to the end of pretence. She would have known that anyway from the rapid beating of her heart, the warmth that pervaded her.

It was slightly shocking to discover that she

could want a man for sex alone, but she couldn't even deny it to herself, although she made one last desperate attempt.

'It wasn't the only reason I pushed you away,' she said in a low voice. 'You spoke once of freedom and said that only I could know what it meant to me. For eight years I was Ben's prisoner, hedged in by his petty, spiteful demands that controlled my life. Now I'm free of him, but there's more than one kind of prisoner—'

'But I don't want to be your gaoler,' he said, understanding her at once, 'only for us to find a new kind of freedom together. Trust me.'

The last words were full of perils, but he swept them away by simply laying his mouth over hers. For a moment they were both still, then his lips moved, not demanding but coaxing, teasing. That was her undoing. She could have resisted arrogance but gentleness lured her on, so that she moved her own lips in response, teasing in her turn, sensing his response, as helpless as her own.

She felt his arms go around her so that her head fell against his shoulder and he was kissing her in a way that was almost old-fashioned, as part of an enveloping embrace. It was natural to put her own arms about him and let her hand find its way to the back of his neck, caressing it with longing. Her lips fell apart and his tongue invaded her, moving with subtle skill, as though he'd been here before and knew all about her.

Once before, in the nightclub, she'd seen him as the devil, and now the thought was there again, for how else could he have known that the flickering of his tongue in just that spot could send scurries of pleasure through her? Or perhaps it was his unseen presence, living with her like a ghost ever since, and silently learning her secrets.

But after this there would be no more secrets. This was her last chance to run for cover, because once he'd taken possession of her she would be his, irrevocably. Every instinct she had warned her to escape now, while there was still time.

But there was no time. That moment had passed long ago, and now she was merely living out decisions taken deep inside her, in the still of the night.

He took her hand and led her into her bedroom. His fingers were at the buttons of her blouse, that plain garment with which she'd thought to assert her indifference. It vanished easily and his hand was cupping her breast while his lips made a light, burning trail down her neck.

When she reached out for his clothes he helped her, tossing them aside with relief, then quickly removing the rest of hers.

The sight of his nakedness made her realise how much she'd dwelt on the thought in the months since their first meeting. He was different from her expectations—leaner, more lithe, yet still with an air of power that had nothing to do with mere muscles. His arousal was clear now, a stark, unmistakable message, to which her own arousal was the answer.

Vincente drew her against him so that they stood, holding each other gently, as though waiting for something. His face was very close to hers.

'Trust me,' he murmured again and began to lead her to the bed, drawing her down beside him.

Elise reached for him blindly and felt him, hard and purposeful as a weapon in her hand. But he bided his time, kissing her breasts first and then beginning to kiss her everywhere. Now there was nothing she could do but trust him, yielding herself to the fire in her flesh that mounted, consuming her.

He'd promised her tender care and he was keeping his word. The touch of his lips and fingers was gentle, with nothing to alarm her. But now she was such a contrary creature that, far from appreciating his restraint, she felt as if he were torturing her. She wanted more than this—much more—and he was making her wait.

She tried to urge him on, using her hands to incite him. Everything in her screamed, *Please*— but nothing would prevail on her to yield that far. Instead she sent the message with every caress, every flickering touch—a silent demand for pleasure and fulfilment.

Stroking his back, she could just make out his spine, the flexing of his muscles, then the swell of his behind, which she enclosed and drew towards her. Understanding, he reached out to part her legs, but she was ahead of him, welcoming him between them. There was one last moment when she seemed to be poised on the edge of a precipice, waiting to know if she would fly or fall.

She felt him seeking entry—slowly, with devastating control, easing himself in, forward, giving her the time she needed. Little by little he became part of her, gliding in easily because she was moist with desire, ready for him, gladly accepting each new revelation. And suddenly she was soaring into the clear air.

Now he was deep inside her, moving slowly, withdrawing just enough to return, then repeating the movement with renewed power.

The ultimate moment was a revelation, telling her that her body had been made for this. The violence of her pleasure was almost scary, and scarier still was the need to yield to it—fierce, overwhelming. Years of control and caution fell away from her, leaving her free to become the woman she had always been at heart.

Elise gripped him hard, wanting to draw him more deeply into her, to take control of him until he became nothing but an instrument for her delight. When a man was this good, a woman had the right to his services, didn't she? The right to take and demand until she was satisfied. And she would never, ever be satisfied because the craving to feel him inside her, moving fiercely yet subtly, creating pleasure where pleasure had never existed before, was an endless need.

The cry that broke from her as she reached the pinnacle was part triumph, part despair that the end was in sight. She arched upward, her arms about his neck, while they thrust against each other until the moment when they both had to recognise that it was over.

He laid her gently back on the bed, his eyes fixed on her face. His breathing was coming in harsh gasps and his eyes were a little wild. Somehow she sensed astonishment—not in his expression but in his whole body. Whatever he'd expected to find in her bed, he'd found something else.

She let out a yell that was half a laugh, closing

her eyes again, then giving a long sigh of content-
ment. Suddenly the whole world was wonderful.
When she opened her eyes again he was leaning
on one elbow, regarding her with wry interest.

'Who are you?' he asked.

'I don't know,' she cried, throwing back her head
and arching upwards in delight. 'I don't know *and
it's wonderful.*'

'As long as it's wonderful, that's all right,' he said.

'Do *you* know who I am?'

Vincente shook his head. 'No, I no longer have
any idea.'

'No longer,' she echoed, laughing. 'That means
you once thought you did, but you were wrong,
d'you hear?'

'Yes, I was wrong,' he said quietly. 'I was wrong.'

It was in the early hours when Vincente slipped out
into the silent street, got into his car and drove
away in the direction of the River Tiber. At last he
stopped and went to lean over the side, looking out
over the water to where the lights of the Vatican
City gleamed against the dark, like the promise of
blessing in a wicked world.

Regarding the beautiful scene, his heart full of
recent joys, he yet found a darkness inside him
that he couldn't shake off. His flesh still seemed

to burn with the intensity of his desire and hers, and the fulfilment she had offered that had been like no other in his life, but his mind was haunted and troubled.

'*Buon giorno, signore.*'

Lost in his thoughts, Vincente hadn't heard anyone approach. Now he turned sharply and saw a mean-looking, undersized man with sharp, glinting eyes.

'Do I know you?' he demanded.

The man gave a silent laugh. 'Probably not. So many people who hire me choose not to know me later. I respect that, but I do like to check that my work was satisfactory.'

'Oh, yes. You,' Vincente said distastefully. 'Leo Razzini.'

'The same.'

'I did hire you, but it was some time ago.'

'It was a long job and a hard one, but I worked well for you, didn't I? I found the lady and the fat idiot she was married to, and I helped lure him to Rome so that you could offer him a job. It should have been easy for you after that. Pity he had to go and die. Still, you managed to—shall we say?—"persuade" her here in the end.'

'I advise you to shut up and leave,' Vincente said in a hard voice.

'Of course you despise me now. With the job done and the lady in your power, you can afford to despise me. But my work was satisfactory. At least admit that.'

'If this is an attempt at blackmail I warn you to go no further,' Vincente raged softly. 'I have enough friends in the police to have you locked up for years before you could get anywhere near her.'

'*Signore*, please!' Razzini sounded genuinely hurt. 'Blackmail is something I never indulge in. It wouldn't be safe. Some of my customers have made much worse threats than yours, and I know they mean them.'

'Then what the devil do you want?'

'A kind word, perhaps. I live by recommendations. After all, I can hardly advertise my line of work, can I? So if you hear of anyone needing my services, you might put in a word for me. Tell them how many others you put on the job before me, and that I was the one who cracked it. That's all I ask, apart from the very generous fee you paid me. I hope you feel I provided value for money.'

'I have no complaints with your service,' Vincente said harshly.

'It was the right lady that I tracked down for you?'

'Yes,' Vincente snapped.

'I'm glad of that, because it wasn't easy. You couldn't give me much information to go on, but I did my best, and it all fell into place in the end. Don't the English have a saying—all's well that ends well?'

Vincente clenched his hands and thought of murder.

'Shut up!' he snapped. 'Shut up! And if you know what's good for you, clear out and never let me see you again.'

It was disconcerting that her first thought on waking was of Vincente, as though he were still there with her in the bed, still possessing her body. But then she opened her eyes and found that it was day, and the early sun was streaming in, and she was alone.

Elise had a dreamy memory of him kissing her forehead before he left, which seemed strangely formal after what they had shared. But perhaps that was for the best. In the night they had become different people, and that quiet kiss had seemed to mark the return to their daytime selves.

Who would have thought she would return to Italy like this?

When Ben had dragged her away from Rome she could never have foreseen the way she had awoken on her first morning back, yawning and stretching luxuriously in the great bed.

She felt full of vigour, leaping up and plunging into the shower. She breakfasted on coffee, feeling no need of anything else, and hurried to get dressed. Her exhilarated mood had calmed and now she was thinking of Angelo again, wanting to see again the places where they had been together in a time when happily ever after had seemed possible.

He had been twenty, a charming handsome boy and a 'poor student', he'd always claimed, although he'd seemed to do little studying and always had money to spend. Elise had suspected the existence of a well-off family in the background who'd urged him to study, paid him an allowance but took little further interest.

But she'd been too much in love to spend much time puzzling about the discrepancies. He'd loved her. She'd loved him, and their shabby apartment had been a haven where nobody was allowed to intrude.

Before leaving she took out the cellphone Vincente had given her the night before and turned it off. Deeply as he'd affected her, today was Angelo's and she didn't want to be disturbed.

There were a dozen places to visit, but her feet seemed to find their own way through the streets to the great Trevi Fountain. It was as magnificent and beautiful now as it had been then, the great half circle dominated by the statue of Neptune. It was here that Angelo had urged her to toss in a coin and promise never to leave him, or Rome. And she had promised with all her heart.

But the very happiness of the memories made them terrible to face. The young man she had loved was still here, sitting by the water, laughing at her as she hurriedly sketched him. She was clever at drawing and he had told her that she must become a great artist.

'Not me,' she'd protested. 'I can draw well enough for fashion but real art would be beyond my reach.'

It was true, but she had a facility for capturing a likeness. Her picture of him had caught his essence—not just his face but his air of anarchic humour. She remembered how they'd gone back to his room and he'd stretched out on the bed, watching her as she converted the sketch to a water colour. He'd been delighted when she gave him the finished picture.

'I shall have it framed and hung in a place of honour,' he'd vowed. 'Now come here.'

He'd held out his arms for her to join him on the bed, and she'd forgotten the rest of the world.

That had been almost their last happy time. A week later Ben had arrived. Now she wondered if

Angelo really had framed the picture, and what had happened to it.

She stood looking at the water sparkling in the sunlight. Nearby was a young couple, tossing coins, vowing to return to Rome and love each other for ever.

'For ever,' she murmured. 'If they only knew.'

Before leaving the fountain she closed her eyes and spoke to Angelo in her heart.

I'm sorry, she said. *I'm so sorry for what I did to you. I never stopped loving you.*

Suddenly her mind was filled with memories of the night before, when only Vincente had existed, and the warmth began to spread through her body again. She had loved Angelo passionately, but she had been an ignorant girl, with no knowledge of what a man's skill could do for her, the heights to which it could drive her. She knew now that Angelo had been an unskilled boy, but she had loved him truly and never wanted more. Not then.

She shut off the thought. It was a betrayal of Angelo even to think of Vincente at this moment.

I love you, she told him again. *Whatever— whatever happens, you will always be my true love.*

Elise spent the next few hours going around the little cafés where they had been together, pleased to find so many of them still there. But in her heart she knew she was only putting off the moment she didn't want to face, and finally she hailed a taxi and told the driver to take her to Trastevere.

She got out a short distance from the apartment and strolled through streets that had once been familiar to her. They were different, more prosperous. Some of the shops had been updated and when she went inside there were no faces that she recognised, although many of them had been family businesses.

The greatest shock was awaiting her when she came to the little street where the shabby buildings had huddled together. They were all gone and in their place was a building site, crawling with workmen.

'Can I help you?'

The speaker was a middle-aged woman with a cheerful face.

'I was looking for a place where I used to live,' Elise said. 'But it's not here any more.'

'That's right. They're spending money on Trastevere now, bringing it up to date. It doesn't do to be sentimental about the old days.'

'I suppose not. What about the people who used to live in this street?'

'All rehoused. They won't be back. These apartments will cost a mint when they're finished. Whatever was here before has gone for ever.'

'Yes, I can see that,' Elise said quietly.

She walked away. There was nothing to stay for.

CHAPTER FIVE

ELISE found a small café and drank mineral water at a table in the sun while she considered her position. But her brain seemed to have trouble functioning. Even after eight years she had hoped to find someone who remembered Angelo and could tell her how and when he'd died. But now there was only a blank.

She took out the cellphone, wondering if there would be a message from Vincente, but there was only a text from a Signor Baltoni, asking her to call him. She did so and discovered that he was the lawyer Vincente had mentioned, who would be delighted if she would come to see him as soon as possible. They settled on a time that afternoon.

He turned out to be an elderly man with a smiling, grandfatherly appearance.

'I've taken the liberty of obtaining a small bank loan on your behalf,' he said. 'It's not much but it'll keep you going while you decide what you want to do.'

The amount astonished her, so did the low interest rate.

'Didn't they mind letting me have it on such favourable terms?' she queried.

'The bank is always ready to accommodate good customers.'

'But I'm a stranger.'

'Yes—well—er—'

'Somebody wouldn't have guaranteed this for me, would they?' she asked suspiciously. 'Or shouldn't I ask?'

'You shouldn't ask,' he said at once.

She could go storming off to see Vincente, kill the whole arrangement, or she could keep quiet and let things take their course. Of course, there was no real choice. She must tell Vincente firmly that she couldn't accept this.

A soft breeze reached her through the open window. As if in a dream, she rose and went to look out over Rome, for this place was high up on the fourth floor. In the distance she could see the glint of the river, and the gentle grace of St Peter's. Below her, the trees of the Borghese Gardens fluttered in the slight wind and a bird on one of the topmost branches burst out with a song of summer.

'Fine,' she said, turning back. 'Then I won't ask.'

He beamed with relief and after that everything

went smoothly. When she emerged into the sunlight it was with the realisation that she was sufficiently prosperous to live up to her address. It also dawned on her that she had somehow crossed a line and agreed to stay in Rome—at least for a while.

At Signor Baltoni's suggestion, she looked up a small domestic agency which operated from the basement of the building where she lived and arranged for some part-time staff to care for the apartment. That was a relief as its size had daunted her.

With her own front door shut behind her, she allowed herself to consider clothes.

I need some more and now I can afford them, she mused.

Vincente would be in touch soon and they would spend another evening together, and perhaps another night. Pride demanded that she look her best. For tonight she had one dress that would do, and tomorrow she would seek out others.

Elise took it out, giving it a good shake, deciding that it needed ironing if she were to wear it tonight. Vincente was bound to call at any moment.

Right on cue, he called.

'Did your meeting with Baltoni go well?' he asked.

'Very well, thank you.'

'Am I in trouble for interfering?'

'I guess you're not.' She laughed.

'Good. I only want you to find Rome a pleasant place. When I return I shall try to persuade you that it is.'

'Return?'

'Yes, business calls me away. I have to go to Sicily for a few days. But, before I go, will you tell me—is all well with you?'

'Yes, all is well with me.'

'Good. Then I will call you when I return, but not until then. I know you think I can be rather overbearing, so I'll leave you in peace until I'm back. Goodbye.'

'Goodbye,' she said slowly, hanging up.

Elise refused to pine for Vincente. That would be to give him too much importance, she assured herself. There was work to be done, public records to be consulted, seeking Angelo's death certificate.

But several days' searching revealed no Caroni who had died around that time. He might never have existed. In despair, she almost wondered if she'd dreamed the whole thing.

Refusing to give up, she set out to perfect her Italian, partly by watching the television for hours, and partly by reading everything she could lay her hands on. She bought several daily papers and read them over coffee in a small garden restaurant a few doors down from her apartment.

She found that her Italian came back to her easily, and from the simpler papers she moved on to the financial publications.

As Vincente had told her, the Farnese corporation was huge. His grandfather had founded it, his father had tended it, but the real growth had come about after he'd died and Vincente had taken over. As she went through the newspapers Elise discovered item after item that testified as much to Vincente's ruthlessness as to his business acumen. He seemed to succeed in everything he did.

His home, the Palazzo Marini, was on the outskirts of Rome. Once the home of aristocrats, it had fallen into disrepair when debts had forced the family to move out. His grandfather had purchased it, but it was Vincente who had renovated it, then used it as a conference centre and a backdrop for entertaining.

A search of the Internet revealed pictures taken at these gatherings, showing the restored glory of the Palazzo. Some of them also showed Vincente, magnificent in triumph.

Handsome devil, she thought reluctantly. Phone, damn you!

He'd been gone over a week now, and he'd kept his promise not to trouble her. At least, that was how he'd phrased it, she recalled. She might, if she were cynical, think it was a move in their game of staying one ahead, his way of showing that their night together had passed from his memory. Or his way of pretending that it had.

Did that mean he could read her thoughts, and knew that the memories of their voracious sex haunted her every moment? Did he suspect how she ached for him to return?

If so, he could just forget it.

Elise awoke one night to the ring of her doorbell, sounding as though someone was leaning on it. Flinging on a light robe, she hurriedly opened the door.

'Hello,' he said.

Vincente barely got the word out before she'd pulled him inside, seizing his head between her hands and positioning it where she could fasten her mouth on his. She was the aggressor, driving her tongue between his lips and using it to assault him deliciously. She had wanted this with all her being, and now she was going to make the most of it.

It was she who led the way to the bedroom, holding him tightly in case he tried to escape.

Instead, he got ahead of her at the last minute, pulling her down on to the bed, stripping her night clothes from her while she struggled with his buttons. It took longer than they could bear, but at last they were free and she could draw him across her, opening her legs in welcome and emitting a fierce groan as he entered her.

No tenderness now, but vigour, power, plunging in deep, so driven by his need that he could do nothing but claim her fiercely again and again. This was just how she wanted it. With every movement inside her she groaned, the sound mounting until she exploded with a loud cry.

And still it wasn't over because he stayed as he was, lying on top of her, enclosed within her, while his fingertips wandered over her breasts, teasing the nipples to firm peaks, and she wrapped her thighs about him, imprisoning him for her greater pleasure.

He was tireless, bringing her to climax again and again without weakening, until even his stamina ran out and he rolled away on to his back, gasping.

With difficulty, Elise propped herself up on one elbow and leaned over so that she could rest her head on his heaving chest. She had no strength to do more than that.

After a while their energy revived enough for them to get beneath the covers and go to sleep in each other's arms.

By the time she awoke the sun was up. She lay for a while, drowsily content, only half believing what had happened the night before. Every nerve in her satiated body was relaxed and happy. She looked at his face, half darkened now with shadow, and ran her hand over the slightly scratchy surface, smiling with pleasure.

Sliding out from his arms, she slipped on her robe and went into the kitchen. As she made coffee she switched on the radio, just in time to hear a news item that made her prick up her ears. When she switched off the radio she considered for a moment before finishing the coffee and returning to the bedroom, a smile on her face.

Vincente was awake now, leaning back on the pillows with his hands behind his head.

'I've just heard a really fascinating item of business news,' Elise said. 'Apparently your negotiations in Sicily have hit a bad patch. You were so enraged that you stormed out and returned to your hotel, where you are now incommunicado. No messages can get through to you, and you never come to the phone.'

He grinned. 'Tonio's doing well. He's my assistant, and he has strict instructions to conceal the fact that I'm not there.'

Their eyes met. She didn't have to ask any questions. He'd done this to be with her. She knew that and he knew she knew it.

'How did you get away without being seen?' she asked.

'The hotel has an underground passage. The car took me to the airport, where my plane was waiting. Tonight I'll go back the same way.'

'I see. A shrewd business move. That's very smart.'

'I am very smart, aren't I?' he said, apparently considering this seriously. 'With any luck, the other side will have given in by then, impressed by my stern refusal to negotiate.'

'You'll make any sacrifice for your business, won't you?'

He grinned. 'Come here.'

Elise called the agency to cancel the cleaners and they had twelve perfect hours, undisturbed by the world. She wouldn't have believed herself capable of such recurring passion as she discovered that day. It was as though she'd been given a new body to replace the jaded, disillusioned one she'd had before. No matter how often he reached for her, she was ready for him, vibrantly alive as though the earlier times had never been.

What had happened, she wondered, to the beliefs with which she'd been reared—that sex was only beautiful as a part of love, and that to really enjoy it the two of you must grow close in heart and mind?

What she felt for Vincente was burningly intense, but it wasn't love. Love was the sweet and tender feeling she'd known long ago, never to be repeated. The delirious pleasure she knew in Vincente's embrace was something apart.

Briefly she considered trying to engage him in conversation so that their minds could meet, but the time was passing, and when he touched her she forgot everything else but what he could do to her flesh.

It wasn't love but it was a new life and, for the moment, it was enough.

At last it was time for him to depart, slipping away under cover of darkness and leaving her achingly bereft. After that she listened to the radio, which duly reported the moment that 'the well-known entrepreneur, Vincente Farnese, finally agreed to resume negotiations, much to everyone's relief.'

Three days later he called to say, 'I'm back. Can I come over?'

Once more Vincente took her by surprise, arriving on her doorstep with his luggage and still wearing his travelling clothes. Clearly he'd come straight from the airport, and seemed only half awake.

Elise sat him down at the table, ready for the supper she had prepared. He ate it slowly, occasionally talking about his time in Sicily after his return. She formed a picture of endless conferences, working breakfasts, late night sessions, half an hour of sleep snatched here and there.

'I'm made that way,' he said when she mentioned this. 'I can manage on little sleep taken now and then. It's a great help in my business.'

'Hmm. Well, you look awful,' she said frankly.

'Thank you.'

'Don't mention it.'

'But I'm capable of doing the important things. Let me prove it to you.'

Taking her hand, he led the way into the bedroom. They undressed without preamble and lay down on the bed. Elise was suddenly nervous. It had been so glorious before and she'd spent so much time remembering, anticipating. How could anything live up to those fantasies? He would need to be a superhero, and that was a dangerous way to think of any man.

But her hopes were high as she felt him caress her to draw out her response, although she was almost ready before they began. She ached for this, so when he laid his head against her breast and his hands mysteriously stopped moving, she knew a stab of disappointment.

'Vincente,' she said, giving him a little shake. 'Vincente.'

Another shake made him move—not much, but just enough to show her his face, revealing that her worst fears had been realised.

He was asleep.

At first she wanted to scream her vexation and frustration to the world, but then the sight of his softened features caused a surge of tenderness to go through her. She tightened her arms about him so that he settled into a more comfortable position, still with his head resting on her.

Somewhere in her mind a voice spoke, warning her that this was dangerous. The frantic hurly-burly of sex was something she could manage, and relish. But this treacherous sweetness was too much like the feeling she'd known with Angelo, and which she'd sworn never to know again. It was weakness, and she would no more yield to it than she guessed Vincente would himself.

But as long as they were both clear on that point, perhaps there was no harm in a little indulgence.

She smiled, drawing him closer still.

He slept without moving for three hours, while she felt her heart melt. She had no regrets about losing their passion. Tenderness was a more than fair exchange.

Elise dozed and awoke to discover him already awake, taking up exactly where he'd left off. As she moved against him he raised his head, meeting her eyes and inviting her to share the joke. And it was a joke, the funniest joke that had ever made her gasp with pleasure, so that mirth and passion blended into one, in the sweetest experience of her life.

'Time for the real world,' Vincente sighed as they lay together afterwards.

'And that big shareholders' meeting you've got coming up,' she said.

'How did you know about that?'

'I've been reading the financial papers—purely to improve my Italian, you understand.'

'Naturally.'

'You've got a big fight on your hands, but you're going to face them down.'

'Without a doubt. I learned a lot of useful things in Sicily. When I've processed them I'll be ready. Until then I'll virtually have to live at work.'

'So I'll see you again when your meeting's over—if I can find the time.'

His hand was working between her legs again. 'I think you'll find it,' he murmured.

She didn't argue. It wasn't worth it.

She relished their battle of wits. It added spice to what would otherwise have been a one-dimensional relationship. She knew now that his need to make love to her was as fierce as her own answering need, and surviving until after his meeting was going to test her patience.

So it was a special pleasure when he cracked first.

Elise answered the phone and his first words were, 'Can you ride a horse?'

'Yes, I love riding, but I haven't any gear with me.'

'There's a shop in the Via dei Condotti.' He gave her the name, saying, 'You'll get the best there. How good a rider are you?'

'I like a quiet mount.'

'Fine. I'll collect you tomorrow morning.'

He hung up.

It would have been nice to be able to tell him that for once he'd got it wrong, but when she entered the shop she found it as good as he'd claimed. This was annoying for a brief moment, then exhilarating as she plunged in, emerging with clothes that set off her figure to perfection.

'You don't think the jodhpurs are a bit tight?' she asked cautiously.

'They are certainly figure-hugging,' the assistant conceded, 'but the *signora* can risk wearing what others could not.'

Which was a polite way of saying that they hugged her behind provocatively.

'I'll take everything,' she said.

Vincente was driving his own car when he arrived next morning, having called first to say he expected her to be waiting on the front step.

'Yes, sir, no, sir, three bags full, sir,' she'd recited.

'I beg your pardon?'

'Never mind. English joke. I'll be there.'

'Very good,' he said as they drove away next morning. 'I barely had to pause. That traffic attendant was ready to become very difficult.'

'Difficult with *you*? Nonsense! He wouldn't have dared.'

He didn't reply but, glancing sideways, she saw him grinning.

'I'm amazed you could spare the time,' she observed as they headed out into the countryside. 'Weren't you supposed to be living at the office?'

'Not a good policy. It could make the enemy think I'm worried.'

'Good, good,' she said, nodding. 'You've probably got a photographer at the stables to take a picture showing how relaxed you are.'

'Now that's a trick I missed. Never mind, a man can't think of everything.'

'I thought you prided yourself on being able to do just that.'

He gave a crack of laughter. 'You caught me fairly there.'

After a moment he said quietly, 'I hope you know I wouldn't impose a photographer on you without warning. You might not believe it, but I have enough manners for *that*.'

'You're right,' she said demurely. 'I wouldn't believe it.'

He gave a shout of laughter. 'I'm not that bad, am I?'

'Is this place very far?' she asked wickedly.

'All right, for the moment I'll let you snub me. You'll change your tune when you see your mare. I chose her specially for you.'

'So you think you can dictate that for me as well?'

Vincente grinned. 'Wait and see.'

By now they were out in the country and a few minutes later they turned down a long lane that led to a riding stable. A groom led out an elegant dappled mare and introduced her to Elise as Dorabella.

'But we call her Dora,' he explained. 'She prefers it. She's very friendly. Signor Farnese said she would be just what you wanted.'

And she was. He'd even managed to get this right! But Elise was too preoccupied with stroking Dora's nose and receiving a nuzzle in return to take exception.

Vincente's mount was a magnificent stallion called Garibaldi, with fire in his eyes and impatience in his step. They set out together, but soon Elise sensed that Vincente and his mount were equally impatient to let rip.

'Why don't you take the edge off him first?' she said. 'I'll go at a more gentle pace.'

He was away like the wind, while she took Dora up on to a slight incline from where she could watch him. Garibaldi leapt, soared and pounded the ground with a fierce vigour that echoed that of the man on his back.

Now they were out of sight, but after ten minutes she saw them again in the distance, racing with an exuberance that was almost violent.

'I'm glad we didn't go in for any of that,' she told Dora, stroking her neck. 'Why don't we—*oh, no!*'

The cry was wrenched from her as Garibaldi soared over a fallen tree, then faltered, twisting in the air and hurling Vincente to the ground before heading down after him. For a terrible moment her inner eye saw the horse's bulk landing on Vincente and crushing him to death. It seemed that nothing could prevent it, but then, with a mighty effort, Vincente managed to throw himself out of the way of the animal, then collapsed.

Elise galloped to where he was lying on his face, frighteningly still. She jumped from Dora's back and knelt beside him, but he didn't move.

'Vincente!' she cried frantically.

A groan was the only answer, but then, to her intense relief, he gave vent to a stream of curses as he began to push himself up with his arms.

But almost at once he gave up the effort and rolled on to his back.

'You're badly hurt,' she said worriedly. 'I'm going to get an ambulance.'

'No ambulance,' he said, suddenly fierce. 'I don't want anyone to see me like this. Where are the horses?'

'There,' she said, pointing. Garibaldi had survived the fall unhurt and was nibbling grass, with Dora close by.

'Take them back to the stables,' Vincente told her, speaking in painful gasps, 'and fetch the car here.'

He could hardly move but as she made to get to her feet his hand shot out and gripped her.

'No ambulance,' he repeated. 'You tell nobody. Promise.'

'I've got to tell them the horse fell. He might need treatment.'

'Him, not me. Promise.'

'I promise—for the moment.'

Elise pulled free and ran to the horses, mounting Dora and taking Garibaldi's reins. Back at the stables, she handed the animals over with a brief explanation, then ran for the car and in a few minutes was on her way back. She was frantic with fear lest he should have collapsed completely.

She found him sitting on a large stone, where he'd evidently dragged himself with a good deal of pain. He was clutching his side and gasping but managed to force a smile when he saw her stop the car close to him.

'What did you tell them?' he grumbled, grimacing.

'Never mind that now. Put your arm around my neck. It's only a couple of steps.'

She helped him stagger to the car and stretch out on to the back seat.

'What did you tell them?' he repeated.

'Just enough to make sure they got a vet for Garibaldi. I said you had only a few bruises.'

'Are you sure?' he demanded suspiciously, clutching the back of her seat and hauling himself up.

She lost her temper. 'Sure I'm sure,' she yelled over her shoulder. 'They asked why you weren't coming back and I said it was because you were a miserable, ill-tempered so-and-so who couldn't bear anyone to see him when he looked silly. They accepted that without question.'

He gave a grunt. 'Fine.'

'I'll have you home in a minute.'

'Not my home,' he said quickly. 'Yours. I don't want to be seen by anyone who knows me. Just let word get around that I'm in this state and the jackals will start closing in on me.'

'All right.'

Vincente collapsed back into his seat and said no more until they reached home, where he forced himself to limp to the lift without help, except for holding her hand. Through that contact she could feel the effort it cost him. He was trembling and the sweat stood out on his brow, and it was a relief when the doors opened to reveal nobody in the corridor and she was able to get him inside her apartment, unnoticed by anyone. There he collapsed again on to the sofa.

'You need a doctor,' she said.

'I told you—no.'

'Why all this mad secrecy?' she demanded, exasperated.

'It's not mad, it's essential. You know about the shareholders' meeting, how important it is. There are going to be arguments that I have to win. I've got to be at my best, no sign of weakness.'

'Too bad if you pass out,' she snapped. 'Of course they may not take that as a sign of weakness.'

'Heaven save me from a managing woman!'

'Heaven save you from your own stupidity! Vincente, listen to me. I'm not going to argue. You need treatment and I'm going to call someone, either a doctor to come here or an ambulance to take you away. Your choice.'

He glared at her. 'You're making a fuss about nothing.'

'When a doctor tells me that, I'll believe it. What's your doctor's number?'

'Elise—'

'It's that or the ambulance, and you have ten seconds: nine, eight—'

'*All right!* I'll call the doctor myself—' he yelled, before muttering under his breath, 'so that you don't make it sound as though I'm dying.'

'Hah!'

'What does that mean?'

'It means I'll say what I want to when he gets here and you won't stop me.'

'*Cane dei to morti!*' he raged.

'Anything you like,' she said, recognising the curse. It had been one of Angelo's favourites, and was an extremely rude comment about ancestors and their likely burial sites. 'Now get on that phone.'

He did so, scowling at her in a black rage.

'He'll be right along,' he growled at last, hanging up.

'I'll help you get undressed and into bed.'

'Thank you,' he said in a quieter voice.

'Why have you stopped snarling at me?'

'Because you weren't taking any notice,' he admitted wryly.

'Then you're quite right not to waste time on it. Put your arms around me and I'll help you up.'

Vincente made no further argument, but allowed her to take him into the bedroom, where she stripped him down to his underpants and settled him in bed.

'I'm sorry I shouted at you,' he said at last. 'Sometimes I'm a bit—'

'I know you are. More than a bit. Lie still.'

The doctor arrived ten minutes later. He and Vincente were old friends and said what they liked to each other. He conducted an efficient examination and snorted. 'You've got off lightly,' he said. 'A twisted ankle and you've pulled a couple of muscles in your back, which probably hurts like the devil but isn't serious. A couple of days in bed should do a lot. I'll send a nurse in.'

'No nurse,' Vincente said at once. 'I don't want strangers.'

'I'll do it,' Elise said.

'Thank you,' the doctor said. 'You'll just have to wait on him generally and be a maid of all work.' He glanced wryly at Vincente, adding, 'If you can stand it, *signora.*'

'Maybe *he'll* have a tough time with *me*,' she said lightly, and received Vincente's wry look of appreciation.

CHAPTER SIX

WHEN the doctor had left, Vincente said, 'You were right.'

'The doctor said it's not so bad,' Elise reminded him.

'It's worse than I wanted to admit. I should have listened to you.' Vincente took her hand. 'Thank you for looking after me, and I suppose I should apologise for dumping myself on you. It never occurred to me to ask first.'

'Now why doesn't that surprise me?' she mused.

'Am I being a pain in the neck?'

'No more than usual. Luckily I have a sense of humour.'

He managed a smile and lay back, grimacing.

'I must call my secretary,' he said. 'There are some files I need her to bring over first thing tomorrow.'

'You don't mean to work?' she demanded.

'I've had one day off, and that's all I can afford.'

'But you're a sick man.'

'Officially I'm not.'

'To hell with officially. You can't move without wincing.'

'The doctor left me strong painkillers. I've had two and they'll start to work at any minute,' he protested.

'If I gave vent to my feelings at this moment you'd *need* even stronger painkillers.'

He regarded her with appreciation. 'You have the makings of a really splendid bully,' he said.

'You'd better believe it.'

Vincente made his phone call, giving a string of orders to his secretary, for whom Elise felt profoundly sorry. She made him a light lunch and went to the bedroom to find him off the phone, looking weary. For a moment his pain was clear, then he saw her and immediately looked cheerful. She wasn't deceived.

'Is it very bad?'

'Not really. The worst thing is feeling like a complete damned fool. What kind of idiot makes such a mess of things?'

'You do things that no other man can do,' she reminded him, smiling.

He grunted with laughter and gasped. 'Please don't make me laugh.'

'All right. Just have something to eat.'

He gave a helpless grimace. 'I'm going to need help sitting up properly.'

She guessed it maddened him to ask, but when she came to the bed he put his hands up around her neck and used her for support.

'Thank you,' he muttered.

'Hey, it's not the end of the world,' she rallied him. 'So you had to accept my help! So what?'

'You're being very reasonable, of course,' he growled.

'But to hell with reasonable!' she said sympathetically.

'Something like that.'

'It's just a pity it had to be your back,' she said. 'It's one of those things that isn't dangerous but hurts like hell. Has it ever happened before?'

'Why do you ask?'

'My father had a bad back. It came and went. He'd have a few good months then some silly thing would make it go again and he'd be in agony. It can strike anyone.'

'If you mean me—nonsense!' he said at once.

'You mean it's never happened before?'

'Once or twice, yes, but—' He stopped and sighed. 'I guess I'm just like your father.'

'In many ways,' she said, amused. 'He hated anyone knowing the truth. He thought it was a

sign of weakness, which was very silly of him,' she
added significantly.

'Not silly at all if the sharks are circling,' he
replied at once.

'And I suppose there are plenty of sharks circling
you? I wonder just how many enemies you have.'

Vincente made a wry face. 'Enough not to want
them to know I have a bad back. Did your father
have many?'

'No, he wasn't a big tycoon. He was a sweet-
natured man who raised me after my mother died.
I was a sickly child and he kept having to take
time off from work to look after me, and so he lost
a lot of jobs.' A fond smile overtook her face. 'He
so much wanted—'

Elise broke off as his cellphone rang. He answered
it with a sound of exasperation and she slipped away.

She left him to work, going back later to collect
the tray. Finding him asleep, she removed everything quietly.

When her bedtime came she sought for a demure
nightie. Not finding one, she settled for an outrageous one and slipped in beside him. The bed was
large enough for her to be several feet away, so
propriety was observed—sort of—but she could
be there to look after him.

He awoke in the small hours and she helped him

to the bathroom, remade the bed, helped him back, and brought him some more painkillers.

'Thanks,' he growled.

'You don't mean thanks,' she said cheerfully. 'You actually hate me because you had to lean on me there and back. Shall I go away?'

His hand closed over hers. 'Stay,' he said briefly.

She pulled the covers up over him. 'Go back to sleep.'

In the morning she helped him again and fed him. Then they had an argument because he refused more painkillers.

'They send me to sleep,' he complained. 'My secretary's coming this morning. I need to be alert.'

The secretary turned out to be a formidable woman, bearing files and a laptop computer. They worked together for a couple of hours, then she left, full of his instructions. Vincente got to work on the laptop and divided his afternoon between that and the telephone.

But at last there came the moment when even he had to agree that enough was enough and take some more painkillers. Even then he fretted about something he hadn't done.

'Forget it,' she said firmly. 'Go to sleep.'

'Will you be here?'

'Just try to get rid of me.'

A grunt was his only reply but it told her all she needed to know, and she smiled as she snuggled down.

In the early hours she awoke to find him still sleeping and went to sit by the window, watching light creep over the city. She felt peaceful for the first time since she'd arrived here.

'Buon giorno!'

He was awake, smiling at her from the bed, and she went straight across to sit beside him.

'Can I get you something? How's the pain?'

'Better, as long as I don't move. I don't need pills just now. Talk to me instead.'

'All right, let's talk about your big meeting and how you're going to slay everyone.'

'No, just for once I'll shut up and listen. Go on talking about your father. You were going to tell me about something he badly wanted, when the phone rang. What was it he wanted?'

'I forget now—oh, yes—he wanted to make a lot of money and give me treats, but there never was any money. As though I cared when I had such a wonderful father.'

'Tell me about him.'

'What I remember most is that he was always there for me, always ready to play games and laugh at silly jokes.'

He grew still, watching her, fascinated by the smile that touched her lips. It was fond and indulgent, containing the whole history of a happy childhood. Vincente thought of his own childhood, and the father he'd rarely seen.

'Go on,' he said.

She found it easy to slip back into that blissful time. A whole host of incidents rose in her mind, crowding each other as she hurried to tell Vincente. Suddenly she was happy, as though her beloved father was there with her again.

'You really loved him, didn't you?' Vincente asked, remembering how she'd gone to visit the grave on the day they'd left London.

'Yes, I did. I wish he were here now, but he died a few months back. If only—'

'If only what?' he asked as she stopped.

'No, it doesn't matter.'

'Tell me,' he urged. Something told him this was important. When she still hesitated, he reached out and touched her gently. He had the feeling that he was on the verge of a revelation.

'I came to Rome to study fashion, and I was so stupid that I never even asked how Dad raised the money to send me here. He told me he'd had an insurance policy that was to pay for my higher education and it matured at just the right moment. I believed him, because I wanted to.

'Of course he'd really borrowed the money at a huge rate of interest, then couldn't afford to make the payments. He was working in Ben's business at the time and some money came his way that he thought he could take without anyone knowing. So he did, and Ben found out.'

'What did Ben do about it?' he asked, with sudden urgency.

'He came out to Rome to tell me what Dad had done, and that he was going to turn him over to the police. I had to stop him, and there was only one way.'

'Are you saying—?'

'Ben wanted me. I was his price. He knew I… He knew I didn't love him, but it made no difference.'

Elise had been on the verge of saying that she loved Angelo, but something stopped her. She still had an uneasy sense of having betrayed her young love with the new feeling that had taken her by storm, and now she couldn't speak of him. Not to Vincente.

'You married Ben—to save your father?' Vincente asked slowly.

'It was the only way. I couldn't let Dad go to

prison, not when it was my fault he was in such a mess.'

She had the feeling that he'd grown suddenly tense.

'And that was why you married that creature?' he asked in a voice with a touch of urgency.

'Nothing else could have made me do it. I know everyone thought I was lucky—a poor girl who'd snapped up a rich man. But I'd never have married Ben if it hadn't been necessary.

'And the real cruelty was that Dad died just two months before Ben did. It could have been so different. If only he'd lived a little longer, we'd have been free together. But it was too late.'

'You're crying,' he said gently.

'No, I'm not. Not really.'

'Yes, you are. Come here.'

Vincente reached out and drew her to him, and she found that she really was weeping—for herself, her father, her ruined dreams. But that it should have happened in the arms of this harsh man, of all people, left her amazed. She tried to stop the flood, even now fearful of yielding a point to him in their battle. But the battle seemed very distant at this moment, and now she could sense a tenderness in him that had never been there before, even in their subtlest love-making.

'Sorry,' she said at last. 'I don't normally give in like that.'

'Perhaps you should. You might cope better in the long run.'

'I cope fine.'

'But you might need some help.'

'I couldn't ever let Ben see me cry.'

'No, he'd have enjoyed it too much,' Vincente said dryly.

'How did you know that?'

'Anyone who ever met him would know that.'

She gave a muffled chuckle.

'What is it?' he wanted to know at once.

'Just that I never saw you as an agony aunt.'

'I have many hidden talents.'

'I'll bet you work to keep that one very well hidden.'

He smiled, but the smile faded as he considered her words. Apart from his mother, Elise was the only person who'd ever seen this side of him. In fact, he'd only dimly been aware that it existed. But in the last few minutes it had come roaring out of its lair to protect her.

Her unhappiness was unbearable to him, but more piercing still were the words she'd uttered a few minutes earlier. She'd married Ben under duress. There had been no soulless pursuit of money, oblivious to who was hurt. She'd done what she had to do for love of her father.

As Vincente leaned back on the bed head, holding her against his chest, he felt a weight being lifted from his heart and, revealed beneath it, was a joy he'd never before allowed himself to recognise.

But he turned his eyes away from that joy. It was too much, too unfamiliar, too complex. He would think about it later.

'You were lucky,' he said. 'To have had a father like that.'

'What about yours?'

'He was a good father in his way, but everything in him was focused on business. He had to dominate and rule, and he wouldn't let up until he had all the power he wanted.'

'Is that why you're the same?'

There was a silence before he said, 'I guess so. It was the way to get his attention. I remember once…'

There in his mind was an incident he hadn't thought of for years; himself, the eager child hoping for praise, his father, impatient of anything that would distract him from his agenda.

So Vincente had countered by becoming the agenda. At school he'd excelled at maths, science, information technology and anything else that might help him become a businessman in his father's image. And it had worked. He'd been taken into the firm and immediately proved himself a chip off the old block.

'Did that make your father proud of you?' she asked.

'Oh, yes, he was impressed.'

'Did that make you happy?'

'It was what I wanted,' he said evasively.

She was too wise to press the point.

Vincente had been given more and more responsibility, had seized it gladly, never seeing the road he was travelling or where it led. When his father had his fatal heart attack Vincente had been, although still in his twenties, ready to take over—ready in all the right ways, and all the wrong ones.

That had been ten years ago, and since then he knew that the qualities he'd started with—an unforgiving ruthlessness, a scorn of weakness, a readiness to duel to the death and give no quarter—had all been emphasised and given a sharper, crueller edge. His presence here with this woman proved it, for reasons that she didn't know and which made him uneasy right now.

That thought made him sit up sharply, so that she almost fell out of his arms.

'Is something the matter?'

'No,' he said quickly, 'it's all right; I can get out of bed. Go to sleep.'

It was painful but he managed. He needed to be alone to think. From the safety of the window-seat he looked back at the bed, where she had closed her eyes, and tried to work out what had happened to him.

It had always been simple. You kept your eye on the target, you did what you set out to do, and if people didn't like it, then tough. If they feared you, that was good. Where women were concerned you played fair, behaved generously, and stayed safe by choosing the kind of woman who understood the game. And you never, ever weakened.

Until now.

He'd been prepared for anything except what had happened to him tonight. Or had tonight merely been the culmination of something that had been creeping up for a long time, creeping so silently that he hadn't seen the danger until it had sprung out of nowhere?

He blamed himself. A good entrepreneur planned for everything and was always ready to fight back. Those were the rules.

But the rules didn't tell you what to do when the desire to fight had drained away, replaced by a treacherous delight in the company of a woman you'd always known was dangerous, and now seemed more dangerous than ever. If he had any sense he'd put a stop to this now, send her back to England and never see her again.

Vincente sat for a long time, watching her as she lay asleep.

They settled into a routine. She nursed and fed him, kept him hidden from the maids on their daily calls, made sure he was always at his best for his secretary's visits, and massaged his back. She'd done this for her father and knew the trick of easing the pain, even if only temporarily.

Sometimes they talked as they had done at the beginning—about childhood, or other things, in a lighter vein.

'I want to hear all about your other women,' she said one night with a chuckle. 'Go on, entertain me.'

They were drinking wine, side by side in bed, propped up by pillows, and he gave her a comical, cynical glance.

'If you think I'm falling into that trap you have a very poor opinion of me. Try again.'

'Shame!' she cried. 'What about that little flat you keep? The perfect place for orgies.'

'That was chosen for its proximity to my office,

so that when work overwhelms me I don't have to go the full distance home,' he said loftily.

'Yeah, right!'

'Well, it's not a home, anyway.' With a sudden note of surprise he said, 'This feels more like home.'

'With me paying slavish attention to your every whim? That's your idea of home?'

'Certainly,' he said with a grin. 'What else?'

She chuckled and spilt her wine, so that she had to dab herself and him.

'How did you know about my flat?' he asked after a moment.

'I told you before, I've been reading about you in the papers.'

'Did they say anything else about me?' he asked in a carefully blank voice, not looking at her.

'Just the same story endlessly recycled—glutton for work et cetera. Since you don't ever seem to give interviews, they're kind of stuck. They just said the flat was handy for your work, almost monk-like in its austerity. I invented the bit about orgies.'

'That's a relief.'

She looked at him impishly. 'So you can relax. They haven't found the true story.'

He returned the look. 'Keep trying. You'll get nowhere.'

They laughed and let it drop. But gradually it

seemed to Elise that he was less willing to talk than he had been. She wondered if his life had been truly unhappy, or whether he was afraid of accidentally revealing professional secrets.

She was discovering that every time she thought she had Vincente's measure he could surprise her again. On the day before the shareholders' meeting he made her a gift that took her breath away.

'Shares?' she exclaimed, bewildered.

'Now you're a shareholder in the firm, so you can attend the meeting,' he explained. 'Call it your nursing fee.'

'But—a few shares, yes—but this is a fortune.'

'You're a very good nurse. Look what you've done for me.'

To demonstrate his point he walked up and down, finishing before her with a flourish.

'All your work,' he said.

Now he could walk more easily, but if he had to stand for any length of time the pain returned and this worried her because she knew he would need to stand a great deal during the meeting.

It wasn't his first trip out. The previous day he'd been to visit his mother, and had managed pretty well. But then he hadn't spent much time on his feet. Today would be different.

'Sit down as much as you can,' Elise was unwise enough to say now.

'Sit down? While my enemies are standing up? I don't think so.'

'Well, take some painkillers first.'

'And risk falling asleep? No way!'

They travelled together in his chauffeured car and parted at the door. Once inside, she found herself escorted to a seat at the front, clearly on his instructions. Elise was prepared for the worst and found the meeting as stormy as she'd expected. She had very little idea of what was going on because her Italian couldn't cope with the furious invective that came up from the floor and back from the platform. She only knew that Vincente was being attacked, and was attacking back in fine style.

Watching him carefully, she could see the moment when the pain began, but she doubted if anyone else would notice. The only outward sign was that he became more aggressive, more determined to crush opposition. Even with her limited understanding, it was clear to Elise that he was dominating the meeting, persuading everyone to his point of view or, if not actually persuading them, leaving them no choice but to do it his way.

It wasn't amiable but, like everything else about him, it was exciting.

Afterwards, she lingered as he came down the steps from the platform. People crowded around to shake his hand and it seemed to her that every shake made him wince, although he never lost his smile or his air of assurance.

Then, to Elise's dismay, someone clapped him heavily on the back, insisting that they must all have a good lunch to celebrate.

'I'm afraid not,' Vincente said, maintaining his smile by sheer will-power. 'Now the meeting's over there's more work to do than ever.'

'But you got your way.'

'That's why there's work to do. You go to lunch. Ah, there you are.'

He seemed to become aware of Elise for the first time, although she was sure he'd seen her. As she came forward he slipped an arm about her shoulders.

'Let's go,' he said.

To the others it looked merely as though he was walking away with a beautiful woman. Only Elise knew that he was leaning on her heavily.

His car was waiting outside. As he settled down in the back seat, closing his eyes, Elise produced the painkillers and a small flask containing mineral water, handing them over in silence. He nodded and swallowed thankfully.

He must have given the driver her address in

advance, because they headed straight there, reminding her what he'd said about it feeling like home.

Elise didn't speak until the front door was safely shut behind them, then said firmly, 'Get undressed, go to bed and I'll give your back a rub.'

She joined him a few minutes later, pulling back the sheet to find him naked underneath. The strain was still there in his face, but he relaxed a little as she began to massage him.

'So you won,' she said, beginning to knead the tense muscles.

'Of course.'

'There's no "of course" about it.'

'That is, when I have my confederate looking after me. Thank you. I couldn't have done it without you.'

'Well, I didn't want to risk my shares losing value, did I?'

'Well done. I'll make a businesswoman of you yet.'

But the next moment he winced and she said, 'Stop trying to put a brave face on it. I'm not someone you need to impress.'

'No, I wouldn't get far trying that, would I? You've seen me at my weakest.'

'But weakness isn't important,' she protested.

'I think it is.'

'No, we're all weak sometimes, in different ways. What matters is how we act when we're well and feeling strong enough to be cruel. Surely that's how you should really judge someone.'

'Are you thinking of anyone in particular?'

'You mean Ben? Yes, of course. But I soon felt that everyone he introduced me to was the same. All cheats and back-stabbers. Every one. Is there one man in a thousand who can actually be trusted?'

'Can't I?' he asked curiously.

'Well, I wouldn't like to take you on in business. I don't think you'd have much scruple about anything you did.'

'But do you trust me as a man?'

After a moment she said, 'I don't really know you, do I?'

'I thought we knew each other very well.'

'Only in one way. When we hold each other and make love—then I seem to know you through and through.'

'But isn't that the best way?'

'No,' she said thoughtfully. 'It's an illusion. I don't really know what's going on inside your head.'

'If it comes to that,' Vincente said after a moment, 'nobody knows anything about anyone else's thoughts. Men and women, we all keep our secrets from each other. Perhaps we need to. You and I—'

he hesitated before going on in a slightly forced voice '—both have things we know about ourselves that the other wouldn't understand, or forgive.'

'Forgive?' she echoed. 'What a curious word to use.'

'Life would be impossible without forgiveness,' he said sombrely. 'And the hardest person to forgive may be ourselves.'

Elise wanted to ask him what he meant by this, for there was some note in his voice that hinted at an untold story. But when she next looked at him he'd closed his eyes.

Later that night she came to join him in bed. From his breathing, he was asleep, lying on his back with the sheet pushed down, so that most of his naked body was revealed.

Wryly, she wished he would wear something. To sleep beside him like this was straining her self control. It was little more than a week that they had been together, yet it seemed like an eternity since she'd been free to clasp him without having to worry about hurting him.

It was annoying that he seemed unaffected by the swift mounting desire that afflicted her. He seemed to have no problem at all controlling himself, but perhaps that was only because he'd been feeling bad.

Gently, not to awaken him, she eased herself
into the bed and put out the lamp, but there was
still enough light in the room for her to discern his
outline. She would be strong and not yield to
temptation, yet even as she vowed this she was
gently pushing back the sheet just a few inches…
just a little more…

At last she saw what she longed to see. Even in
his sleep he was aware of her, wanted her, responded to her. Scarcely breathing, she reached
out to caress him gently with her fingertips,
feeling the tremors that went through her. She
must draw back now, before it went too far…

'Don't stop there.'

She gave a little gasp and turned to find him
grinning.

'How long have you been awake?'

'It's hard to be certain. I came up from the
depths into a delightful dream of you doing what
I've been wanting for days. I'm still not sure which
is dream and which is reality.'

'Let me help you,' she whispered.

She began moving her hand again, but pur-
posely now where she had been gentle before,
and had her reward as he grew hot and hard in her
hand. At any moment she was sure he would toss
her on to her back and climb over her, but instead

he lay there watching her with a smile of satisfaction on his face.

'I guess I'm going to have to do all the work.' She chuckled. 'You really fancy being some Eastern potentate being ministered to by the harem, don't you?'

'You forget I have a bad back,' he reminded her. 'I mustn't do anything that would tire me.'

'Hah!'

'But I admit I like the harem idea.' He grinned. 'So get on with your work and pleasure me, wench.'

'To hear is to obey, master.'

She applied herself to the task with a will, watching his face where she could clearly see that he was fighting the temptation to reach for her. They were laughing as they contended with each other, each balancing seduction with control, struggling for supremacy in the battle that gave spice to their relationship.

He partly yielded, stretching out his hands in the direction of her breasts, but she teased him by staying just out of reach.

'Not...fair,' he complained in a gasp.

'All right, I always fight fair,' she said, leaning forward just enough for his fingertips to caress her nipples and almost shouting aloud as the electric tremors went through her, seeming to pulverise her, making her fight for control. To her delight she managed to hold her own, still the one in charge—just.

'You're cheating,' he groaned.

'How? Did you like that?'

'Yes, do it again!'

'How am I cheating?'

'Taking advantage of an injured man. I could really hurt myself, moving too much.'

She muttered a soft curse at herself for being so carried away that she'd forgotten that. Leaning down, she lay against him and promptly found herself tossed on to her back and her legs parted by a determined knee. Then he was inside her, moving powerfully, sending through her a searing excitement that almost made her explode with pleasure.

She just managed to find the strength to gasp, 'Cheat! Liar!'

'Of course. I always win, no matter what I have to do, and you should have known that by now.'

She made a wild sound as he drove into her, then again. She tightened her arms around his neck lest he should have any insane idea of getting free, thrusting back against him with all her might.

'Do you hate me?' he muttered in her ear. He was laughing.

'Yes—yes, I do—don't stop.'

He increased his power, taking what he wanted without gentleness or consideration or good manners. It was shocking, but it carried her into a new universe, and she forgave him, she forgave him—oh, how she forgave him!

Much later, as they lay together, exhausted, she said, teasing, 'So much for being ministered to.'

'I'll tell you this,' he murmured in her ear, 'if a potentate had you in his harem he'd dismiss all the others.'

'So I should hope,' she said, sighing blissfully.

CHAPTER SEVEN

WHEN the bell rang the following evening the last person Elise expected to find standing there was Mary Connish-Fontain. Since the day she had confronted her at Ben's funeral Elise had barely given her another thought. When there was no news of a DNA test she'd shrugged and forgotten it.

'Aren't you going to ask me in?' Mary demanded as Elise gazed at her, nonplussed.

She stood back for Mary to saunter past her, moving slowly to give herself time to take in her extravagant surroundings.

'Nice,' she said. 'Very nice. And to think you tried to plead poverty. Oh, you're here, are you?'

She'd noticed Vincente, stretched out on the sofa. He gave her a relaxed grin, but his eyes were alert.

'What do you want?' Elise said.

'You know what I want. My fair share.'

'Weren't you going to have a test done? Where are the results?'

'Oh, tests, what do they prove?' Mary said with an attempt at a laugh.

'Everything if they're positive,' Vincente observed. 'Yours wouldn't have been, which is why you decided not to have it. Very wise.'

'Test, test! Who cares about that? Ben always said he'd see me right. I'm only here to get justice.' Her tone became wheedling. 'We both suffered from Ben's little ways. We're both women, surely we can find a way to help each other?'

Elise was beginning to feel light-headed. This conversation was rapidly becoming surreal.

'Each other?' she queried. 'You see us becoming bosom pals?'

'We haven't all been as lucky as you,' Mary snapped. 'You've followed the money wherever it led, haven't you? And you've ended up here. But what about me? Ben promised to marry me.'

'That would have been a little difficult,' Vincente observed mildly.

'Oh, it's easy to see whose side you're on,' Mary snapped. 'It didn't take her long to bring you to heel, did it? That's how she is with men.'

'It's certainly how she was with me,' Vincente agreed, giving Elise a wicked look that almost made her burst out laughing.

'I think you should leave now,' he added. 'And don't bother this lady ever again.'

'I've got my rights,' Mary shouted. 'She should have divorced him.'

'So I would have done, with pleasure, if he'd let me,' Elise told her. 'But he wouldn't. Ben let you down the way he let everyone down. Do you think anything you can say will trouble me?'

'It might, if it was printed in a magazine. I've had offers—'

'Then take them,' Elise said promptly. 'Take the money, say what you like. As if I care!'

'You'll care when I tell them what he used to say about you—that you were a cold-hearted bitch who didn't bother who you hurt as long as you got what you wanted.'

'I dare say he was right,' Elise said coolly. 'I'm a cold-hearted bitch, which means you haven't a hope of moving me. You'd better go now.'

'Ben told me a lot more than you think, all about that Italian boy you were supposed to love, but you dropped him fast enough when you smelled Ben's money. He stood under your window and screamed for you not to betray him, and you just laughed at him. He'd been useful, hadn't he? You used him to make Ben jealous, and you didn't care what happened to him when—'

She stopped, suddenly scared by what she saw in Elise's eyes.

'Get out,' Elise said softly. 'Get out, now.'

Mary fled.

Elise folded her arms across her chest as if holding on to something.

Vincente reached for her but she pulled away.

'You're shaking,' he said. 'Tell me about it.'

She shook her head urgently. Just as before, she wanted to tell him about Angelo, but somehow she couldn't get the words out. It was a sacred subject, not to be raised with the man who'd stolen her heart away from her young love.

'Nothing…nothing…'

'It can't be nothing if it upsets you like this. What was she talking about? Who was that young man?'

'I can't…I can't…'

'I wish you trusted me enough to tell me,' he said sombrely.

She looked into his face, longing to take this final step. Instead of urging her with words he kissed her gently, then again.

'What's so terrible that you can't talk about it?' he asked.

'I can never talk about it,' she said violently.

'Even with me? Is there nothing between us but what we do in bed?'

'I don't know,' she said wistfully. 'Sometimes I've thought so, but those times are so beautiful I forget everything else.'

He nodded. 'It's the same for me, but when I try to reach out to you I've often had the feeling that you're drawing away, as though you want to keep me separate from the things that really matter to you.'

'Don't reproach me—there are things I can't tell even to you.'

He didn't answer in words, but he gave her a look of such unutterable sadness that her heart ached.

'I've never talked to anyone about it,' she begged.

'Did you love him very much?' he persisted. 'Should I be jealous?'

'It was a long time ago. I was another person. At eighteen you love differently, with all of yourself. You haven't learned about caution.'

'And you'll never love like that again. That's what you're warning me, isn't it?'

'I guess so. I loved Angelo more than my life, and he loved me. We wanted to be together for ever, but I had to leave him for Ben. We only had three months before Ben dragged me away. Ever since then I've heard his voice in my head, crying to me not to leave him.'

'What happened to him?'

'He died. I don't know how, but when I tried to call him a woman answered and screamed that he was dead. I can't find out any more.'

'Why didn't you want to come back to Rome? I'd have thought you'd have been glad to.'

'I couldn't face him,' she said simply.

'Face him? But he's dead.'

'Not for me. Sometimes it's as though he didn't die at all, but he's waiting for me somewhere. I know that's partly because we were at a great distance, and I know nothing of the details. It's almost as though his death had no reality, and I was afraid to challenge that.'

'You were trying to keep him alive?'

'Maybe it's something of the kind. Although, when I went back to Trastevere and found everything destroyed, a woman said what had been there was gone for ever, and I knew it was true.

'I tried to learn more about how it happened. I studied the death certificates for that time, but there was nothing in the name of Angelo Caroni, and I don't understand that. Vincente? Vincente?'

Something strange had come over him. He was still holding her, but it was as though he'd turned to stone and she wondered if he could hear her.

'Vincente?'

He seemed to come out of a dream and his

manner was forced. 'You may not have been looking in the right place.'

She gave a wan smile. 'Maybe I've never looked for Angelo in the right place. Perhaps there is no right place, and no man could be as I remember him.'

'Then perhaps you should let him go.'

'I try, but it's as though I'm waiting for something to happen. I don't know what, but I'll know when it does.' She kissed him. 'Thank you for listening. I should have told you before.'

'It's late. We should go to bed,' he said quietly.

Once in bed he held her and gave her a gentle kiss, but didn't try to make love to her. Elise wondered if perhaps she should have kept the story to herself. Was it possible that he was jealous?

She looked up, but he pressed her head against his shoulder.

'Go to sleep,' he said.

He was glad she couldn't see him clearly at this moment, in case his eyes were too revealing. Elise had told him the secret that tormented her, but his own secret was becoming too burdensome to hide.

Next day Vincente left for good and the apartment felt bleak and empty. Half an hour of wandering around it alone was enough to bring Elise to a decision and send her out to pick up a cab. She was away for several hours and arrived back with her arms full of folders.

A text from Vincente announced that he would pick her up at eight that evening, belatedly adding, 'if that's all right.'

He looked surprised when he arrived at the apartment.

'I thought you'd be dressed up and ready to go out.'

'Sorry. I meant to be, but I got reading and forgot the time.'

'It must have been fascinating.'

'It was. Look.' She showed him the folders. 'They're from the place I was studying fashion when I was here before. I'm going back.'

'You mean as a pupil?'

'Yes. The current term will finish next week but they're going to let me join the lessons, just to see if I can still fit in. Then I'll enroll properly for next term.'

Vincente browsed through the papers while she hurried to get dressed. When she returned he was frowning, but he said nothing until they were settled in a restaurant in the next street.

'You don't need to do this now,' he said.

'But I want to. I can't live a useless life. I need to be busy. I'm going to see the estate agent and insist that he makes a real push to sell the apartment, so that I can find something smaller. Then I can have some sort of life of my own.'

'Are you going to have any time for me?' he asked satirically.

'I'll make a little time,' she teased. 'If you're good.'

'Good?'

'I meant virtuous.'

'Oh, you meant that, did you?' he demanded sardonically.

'Now, what else could I possibly have meant?'

'Eat up, you little shrew.'

Afterwards they strolled back to the apartment, but at the street door he said thoughtfully, 'I suppose this is the moment when I kiss you virtuously goodnight and go home.'

'You do and you're dead.'

Laughing, they went up together. The lovemaking was delightful and satisfying, but she thought she detected in him a kind of wariness.

'Why do you keep looking at me like that?' she asked.

'I keep wondering what you're thinking of. Me, or your new career?'

'Anyone would think you were jealous.'

'Let's say I'm possessive. I want you to myself. Jealousy is for people too weak to do anything about it. Don't ever expect me to behave like a gentleman and bow out. Because, I warn you, I'm no gentleman. Never try to brush me aside.'

She gave him a considering look. 'Is that what I'm going to do?'

'You might be foolish enough to try.'

'And if I did?'

'I wouldn't let it happen.'

An awkward imp made her say, 'But suppose I really wanted to drop you? That would be my decision.'

'No, *cara*. When and where it ends between us is my decision. Never forget that.'

His voice was soft, and in that very softness she thought she detected a hint of menace. The imp grew annoyed.

'Are you saying that you'd try to force me?'

'That depends on how you define force. Let's say that I'd make you change your mind.'

'And when I'd said the right words—'

'I'm not talking about words. You would have to really change your mind, really want me, because I'd be satisfied with nothing less.'

'Good grief, you're sure of yourself,' she snapped. 'Suppose one day things don't work out to suit you?'

Vincente didn't answer in words. He simply took her hand, turned it over and laid his lips against her palm. She tried to pull away but his grip, while seeming gentle, was unbreakable. His breath was like a furnace, and his lips tickled her softly so that insistent tremors went through her hand, up her arm.

Yet, even as she responded, she knew that there was something here that was alarming. This wasn't love or even desire, but a simple demonstration of power. He wanted her to know that he held her prisoner, not with locks and chains, but simply by subverting her own will, making her flesh act in defiance of her mind. And, if he could do that, then he was her master indeed.

She must escape him.

She did so, sliding off the bed and reaching out for her robe, but before she could touch it, it was whisked away, tossed into a corner, and his fingers surrounded her wrist.

'Let go of me at once,' she said breathlessly.

'I only want to talk,' he said, still holding her. 'There are things we need to get straight between us.'

'I said *let me go.*'

He ignored her and leaned back, drawing her slowly but inexorably towards him. It was unnerving that such a light grip could be as unbreakable as steel, but there was nothing she could do. When she reached the bed he put his other arm about her waist so that she was forced to sit beside him, unable to move.

'Don't fight me, Elise,' he murmured. 'Don't ever fight me. You can't win. I won't let you.'

'It won't be up to you,' she said through gritted teeth.

He smiled then, and it almost frightened her. There was no amusement behind it, only a kind of sardonic pity.

'Don't fool yourself about that,' he said. 'What happens is always up to me.'

'Never,' she snapped. 'You don't own me and you don't control me.'

'Really?'

'You're deluding yourself. Let me go at once.'

He ignored her, pressing her back on to the bed with his hand on her shoulder. It was the lightest of touches, with barely any pressure behind it, yet when she tried to escape, she couldn't. This was like everything else he did, she thought wildly. Determined, calculated—whether it was taking over a company, silencing an enemy or subduing a woman. He was watching her with shadowed eyes, dark enough to swallow all feeling. She could sense only his unrelenting purpose.

When he was sure that she knew resistance was useless, he let his hand drift away from her shoulder towards her breasts, already peaked and firm in readiness for him. Deny it as she might, she was aching for his caress, but when it came it was light, brushing carelessly over first one breast, then the other, almost as though he hadn't noticed their message.

She lay looking up, furious at her own nakedness and his, more furious still at the fact that her chest was rising and falling with renewed desire, and that there was no way to hide it from him.

He'd only just left her body, she thought, enraged. Just a few minutes ago she had felt satiated, yet with a look and a word he had brought her back to the edge, tense with frustration, raging for the feel of him inside her again, filling her with his power. And he knew it, damn him! He knew everything.

He dropped his head and let his lips trail across her flesh so that wherever he went she was aflame. Then she felt the flickering of his tongue and a groan burst from her, despite her best efforts to silence it, and she raised her hands to her head, digging the fingers into her hair, and arching her back.

Then she realised that he was changing her position, turning her over on to her front and running his hands along her spine. His mouth followed them, while his hands slid down to caress her behind. Her back was tingling as never before. It was a good feeling, yet she wanted to turn over and face him. This position made her so helpless.

Then she forgot everything but what he was doing to her, and how good it felt. Suddenly she let out a sound that was almost a cry. He'd discovered a place at the back of her neck that sent fierce, hot sweetness forking through her. No man had ever touched her there before, and she'd never dreamed that it was a special sensitive place until Vincente discovered it.

He kissed her there with lingering skill, while she lay shaking. Then he gently turned her over, watching her, to know whether his moment was here.

Let it happen, Elise thought crazily. It would be his victory but she no longer cared. Let him have the triumph of claiming her, feeling her enclose him avidly, frantic for what only he could give.

Everything in her longed to scream, *Now!* She just managed to hold it back, but her will was melting into compliance. She wanted him on top of her, inside her, driving her further and faster until she could find the blazing release that was now all she cared about.

Thank goodness he too had reached the edge! She could see his arousal, rising unmistakably from the dark hair between his legs. There was a kind of savage satisfaction in knowing that, like her, he was reacting to the point where control was impossible. She parted her legs, seeking the moment when he had no choice but to enter her and they would become equals in desire and incitement, so that she could conquer him at the moment he conquered her. That would be a kind of sweet revenge.

But instead of settling over her he dropped his head and laid his mouth gently over hers. Incredibly, it was a chaste kiss, almost reverent, lips barely touching.

'Goodnight,' he whispered. 'Sleep well.'

He slid quickly off the bed, picked up his clothes and walked out of the door.

She lay, too stunned to move or to think straight. From behind the door she could hear his movements, and it dawned on her with horrifying force that he'd really gone.

Having inflamed her desire to the pitch of madness, he'd walked away without a backward glance, leaving her unsatisfied and desperate. Determined to show his power over her, he'd done it as coolly and brutally as possible.

'No,' she breathed. *'No!'*

She leapt off the bed and hurled herself at the

door, but even as she wrenched it open she heard the front door close behind him and his footsteps fading outside.

'*No!*' she screamed.

For a blinding moment she was on the verge of rushing after him and hauling him back by force, but mercifully something stopped her. That would be to hand him the ultimate victory—even more satisfying to him than the one he'd already achieved.

Slowly, breathing hard, she made her way back into the bedroom and across to the window. The light was out and she could stand there, unseen. In a moment he strode from the building, went to his car and drove away without glancing up to see if she were there.

Her body was still thrumming with the passion he'd so cynically evoked, while her heart was possessed by hatred. The tension between them almost destroyed her and it was maddening to be unable to do anything except pace the room, hands clenched, fuming.

But there was one thing she could do and she did it, seizing a vase and hurling it at the wall. It made a satisfying crash, but left her feeling no better. She headed for the bathroom and stood under the shower while freezing water splashed over her. It cooled her body, but not her raging heart.

Vincente didn't call her the next day, and her anger grew. Another cold shower helped, but only a little.

On the following day there was a knock on the door, and she opened it to find a lad holding a huge bouquet of red roses.

'Signora Carlton?'

She signed for it, closed the door hurriedly and looked for the note. It was brief:

I have to make a tour of factories and knock some heads together. I'll call you when I get back. Vincente.

'To hell with him,' she muttered. She knew what he was doing—sending her one message in the flowers and another in the curt letter. She knew which was the real one.

She chucked the flowers in the bin.

Now Elise was glad she'd rediscovered the fashion school. She could occupy her brain; she spent several days there, bringing work home and staying up late into the night.

'It'll be wonderful having you back,' the principal said when she officially signed up for the next term. 'I hope you'll make a career of it this time.'

'Don't worry. Nothing's going to stop me.' Under her breath she added, 'Nothing and nobody.'

Every second day another bouquet would arrive, but there were no more notes. Just the blazing beauty of red roses, with their confusing message.

'I know what you're doing,' she said aloud. 'This is how you think to keep me on the hook. You think I'll be confused and worried. You think I'm missing you, dying for you to knock on that door so that I can throw myself into your arms. Think again!'

Always the roses went into the bin, but as the days passed the gesture became less fierce. After a while she began keeping one rose back. Just one could do no harm.

She spent hours going around the best fashion shops in Rome. She'd visited them before, but as a shopper. Now she returned as a student, mentally preparing herself for when term started.

When she wasn't exploring the shops she prac-tised drawing clothes, refining her skills, experi-menting with ideas. She became more and more absorbed until the phone rang one afternoon and at first she didn't hear it.

She finally answered, expecting it to be Vincente. But the voice was feminine and gracious.

'I am Signora Farnese, mother of Vincente,' she said. 'I have heard so much about you, and I can wait no longer to meet you. Will you give me the pleasure of your company for dinner tonight? Vincente is still away, so we shall be quite private.'

'Thank you, I should like to.'

'My car will call for you at seven o'clock.'

Elise dressed with great care, choosing a dress of embroidered ivory silk with a matching jacket, and dressed her hair in a style that was elegant and slightly severe.

The limousine appeared on the dot of seven, and took her on a journey towards the countryside that lay south of the city. It was dusk and the lights were coming on, lighting up St Peter's, glowing in the River Tiber.

There were more lights on the Palazzo Marini when it finally came into view. She'd checked the place out on the Internet, but the reality of the Renaissance building was still breathtaking.

Vincente's mother was a small, bright-eyed woman with a gentle manner and a strong likeness to Vincente. She laughed at Elise's expression.

'Yes, my son takes after me, doesn't he?'

'*Signora,*' Elise said hesitantly, 'how did you know who I was, and where to contact me?'

'I have friends all over Rome,' the *Signora* said with a little smile. 'Some of them were at the shareholders' meeting. Others...' She gave an elegant little shrug.

'Others were everywhere,' Elise finished.

'And they're all terrible gossips. I've never known my son so—shall we say?—absorbed. I knew that I simply had to meet you.'

She spent the least possible time showing Elise around the Palazzo before indicating a short flight of marble steps.

'Up here is my own apartment,' she said. 'Let us go there and be comfortable.'

Her rooms were cosy, with everything on an intimate scale.

'I feel easier here,' the *Signora* said with a smile. 'I get lost in that huge building. I wasn't born to grandeur and I can't really get used to it.'

A small table had been set for supper on a balcony overlooking a view of lavish gardens, with Rome in the distance.

Her hostess treated her royally, serving the very best food and wine. She was in her seventies, and clearly frail, but her gentle manner was enchanting. She seemed to like Elise at once, and was soon confiding in her.

'I thought I would never have a child,' she said. 'My first two babies were stillborn so when Vincente lived it was like reaching heaven.'

'And you never had any others after him?' Elise asked.

'No, but I did have a nephew, my sister's son, who came to live with me after she died. He was—ah, here is our fruit.'

The maid had entered with the next course and the *Signora* was diverted. She seemed to have a butterfly mind that flitted from topic to topic. She asked about her guest and Elise gave a carefully edited version of her life, and an even more discreetly edited version of how she'd met Vincente.

'I'm being very obvious, aren't I?' the *Signora* said at last. 'But I do so long for grandchildren and I'm getting older very fast.'

To Elise's own surprise she was suddenly embarrassed.

'I don't think we can talk about grandchildren,' she said hurriedly. 'Vincente and I are only—'

'Of course, of course. I didn't mean to…let's talk about something else.'

'Yes, let's,' Elise said with relief.

The *Signora*'s words had presented her with something that had been hovering on the edge of her consciousness for some time, without her having the nerve to face it.

She had told herself that she hated him for his treatment of her, but in the last couple of weeks she had missed him abominably, passing from hatred to need to sadness. If he appeared now she knew she would forgive him anything.

And now his mother had held out the prospect of marriage to Vincente, and children. She could no longer deny to herself how much she wanted this.

But it must stay her secret. The battle between them still raged. He might have the upper hand now, but she would still contend with him for pre-eminence. And so it would probably be all their lives.

Was this love? she wondered. It was violent and dangerous—so different from the sweetness she had known with Angelo. Yet it might be love.

Suddenly she became aware that her hostess was addressing her. Lost in her dream, she'd floated away from reality.

'I'm sorry,' she said hastily. 'What did you say?'

'It's getting a little breezy out here. Let's go in.'

Once inside, she hurried to the kitchen to order more coffee while Elise strolled around the room, studying the books and the delightful antique furniture.

Then she saw something that made her heart stand still.

Slowly she moved closer to the wall to get a better view, barely able to believe her eyes.

Hanging there was a small picture, a water

colour depicting the Trevi Fountain with a young man sitting beside it, dipping one hand into the water and smiling at the artist.

It was Angelo.

CHAPTER EIGHT

THERE was no doubt that it was Angelo. This was the picture she'd painted eight years and so many lives ago. She'd given it to him, had always wondered what he'd done with it. Now she knew.

'That was my nephew,' Signora Farnese said from behind her. 'The one I was telling you about.'

Elise whirled to where the *Signora* had reappeared and was watching her sadly.

'Your...nephew?' She could hardly get the words out. A chill had taken possession of her, filling her with dread as she sensed the approach of something terrifying.

It was like being caught in the path of a runaway tank. She could see it about to mow her down, but she couldn't move.

'His name was Angelo,' the *Signora* said softly. 'I raised him and loved him as my own.'

Elise stood quite still, feeling herself turn to ice. It was the only way to cope with what she had learned. Angelo, the young man she had loved so desperately and mourned for so long, had come from this house, had been part of this family? Somewhere, far back in Elise's consciousness, a voice was warning that this was not—*could* not—be coincidence. But she wasn't quite ready to face the implications.

'What…happened to him?' she managed to ask.

'He was the victim of a cruel woman,' Signora Farnese said with a sudden fierce bitterness that seemed to shake her slight frame. 'She killed him.' Hearing Elise's gasp of shock, she hurried on. 'She as good as killed him. He took his own life because he couldn't endure what she'd done to him.'

'He…committed suicide?' she whispered.

She had known that Angelo was dead, but not this.

'What did this woman do to him?' Elise asked in a voice that was almost inaudible.

'She took his love, she made him believe that she loved him in return, but then she abandoned him for another man, a man with more money—or so she thought.'

'I don't…understand.'

'Angelo wanted to be independent, so he rented a small apartment in Trastevere and lived like a poor student. I wonder if she would have jilted him so easily if she'd known that he had a wealthy family behind him.'

'But perhaps she wasn't influenced by money at all,' Elise protested. 'Maybe there was another reason.'

'I never saw the other man, but people who did see him said that he was a bloated, middle-aged pig,' the *Signora* snapped. 'To choose such a one over Angelo—only money could explain it.'

Elise felt as though she were drowning. Fighting to keep her voice steady, she said, 'What did he tell you about her?'

'Very little. Not even her real name. He called her Peri, and he spent almost every moment with her. He would come home for half an hour, rave about his beloved Peri, then vanish again. Vincente and I used to laugh because it was so charming to see a young man so head over heels in love.'

'Vincente…'

'We said it would be the making of him, but it was his destruction.'

'But how? You said he took his life…'

'One day he came to this house, distraught. She'd told him their love was over, but he couldn't really believe it. That night he returned to the apartment they shared, hoping to hear her say that it had all been a mistake, that she still loved him. But the other man was there; he saw them in the window, embracing—the other man taunted him...'

She broke off and closed her eyes.

Elise couldn't speak. She could only stare at the other woman with mounting horror as she replayed the scene that had haunted her nightmares for years.

'I heard this afterwards,' the *Signora* resumed, 'from other people who lived nearby and saw everything. Angelo stood in the garden below the window where she was. The neighbours heard him pleading with her, begging her not to betray him, and they saw her in the arms of the other man, letting him cover her with kisses, revelling in her disgusting behaviour.

'When Angelo couldn't bear it any longer he ran away and drove off in his car. That was the last time anyone saw him alive. He crashed the car. They had to pull him from it, but he was already dead.

'And shall I tell you something else about that evil woman? According to the neighbours, she left Rome that night, without waiting to know what had happened to Angelo. So many times she said she loved him—he told me that—and yet she didn't look back once.'

'Not once?' Elise faltered. 'Surely she called him—?'

'Perhaps she did. Some woman called the flat

while I was there clearing out his things a week or so later. I told her he was dead, but I didn't know who she was. I hope it was her. I hope she knows what she did. I hope it torments her for ever and breaks her heart, but I know she had no heart to break. She murdered him, but she doesn't care.'

Elise felt as though a terrible clamouring filled the air. This moment had been lying in wait for her for eight years, and now that it was here she was without defences.

She didn't know how long she stood there, but at last some quality in the silence warned her that everything had changed. Slowly she turned and found Vincente standing in the doorway, watching her with an expression of stone.

In that moment she knew everything. Her head was full of voices, screaming with denial, but it was useless. She knew.

'Vincente, my dear boy!' his mother cried in delight. 'You didn't tell me you were coming home.'

'It was a last-minute decision, Mamma,' he said. 'I wanted to surprise you.'

'It's the nicest surprise I ever had.' She gave him an eager hug. 'I'll go and order you some supper.'

She swept out, leaving them alone.

If Elise had had any doubts, his face told her the worst. She walked towards him and spoke quietly.

'You knew. You've known who I was all the time.'

He didn't reply in words, but he nodded. She stared at him, stunned. Her sense of betrayal was terrifying, blotting out everything else, but she knew she must struggle to keep calm. This was only the beginning.

'I never dreamed,' she whispered. 'But I should have done, shouldn't I? It's so obvious when you know the missing detail.'

'Elise—'

'Angelo was your cousin.'

'Hush!' he said urgently. 'Don't let my mother hear you. She has no idea who you are, and she mustn't know. I didn't mean you to meet like this.'

'You didn't mean us to meet at all, lest I find out what you've been up to. I've been like a puppet dancing to your tune, haven't I?'

'There's more to it than that. Wait until we've talked and don't let my mother suspect, that's all I ask.'

The *Signora* came bustling back with the news that his supper was on its way.

'Just a snack, Mamma,' he said quickly. 'I have little appetite. I should take Elise home.'

'Nonsense, my dear. Elise isn't ready to go home. Now sit down while I bring you something.'

They had no choice but to obey her although the

strain was written on both their faces. Almost singing with delight, the *Signora* placed food and coffee in front of her son and sat watching him possessively while he ate it.

'Did your trip go well?' she asked.

He forced himself to smile and reply. 'So well that I felt able to return early.'

Elise wondered how he could manage that smile, that almost normal tone. But then she remembered that he was totally heartless, without feelings of his own and oblivious to those of others. How else could he have held her in his arms, speaking words of passion while secretly scheming against her?

Everything she'd thought was between them was compromised by the secret he'd been keeping. From the first moment, not one word he'd spoken to her had been true.

From the very first moment…

The pain was almost unbearable, but from somewhere she drew on reserves of courage to match his performance. If he could deceive, so could she. At all costs she would protect this sweet, elderly woman who had welcomed her so warmly.

So Elise said a few things that she could afterwards never recall, sounding as cheerful as possible, even managing a smile, while inside she was dying.

To make things worse, the *Signora* beamed from one to the other, clearly expecting matters to resolve themselves happily soon.

At last it was over. Vincente rose, declaring that he would take her home.

'There's no need,' she said. 'I can get a taxi.'

'I will take you,' he said firmly.

'Of course,' his mother said, kissing his cheek and adding in a stage whisper, 'there's no need to hurry back.'

They drove in silence until they reached her apartment, and then sat for a moment as though neither could find the strength to move.

'Let's go inside,' he said at last.

'I'd rather you left,' she told him quietly.

'Don't judge me until you've heard what I have to say,' he said in a hard voice.

They didn't speak in the lift, or as they entered the apartment. Elise threw aside her jacket and shook her hair loose, wishing it was as easy to free herself from the recent events of her life.

'You knew my connection with Angelo from the start,' she said, like someone still trying to explain the facts to herself. 'Before you came to England.'

'Yes, I knew.'

Vaguely she recognised that there was something wrong with his voice. He didn't sound like a man triumphant at the success of his schemes. He sounded as though tonight had left him feeling as stunned as herself.

Then she pushed the thought aside. She couldn't afford any weakening.

'How did you find me?'

'I employed an investigator.'

'My God!'

'I knew almost nothing about you, even your real name. Angelo only ever called you Peri. The night Ben went to Trastevere he barged into the flat and barged out again without telling anyone his name. Afterwards I went through those rooms with a fine-tooth comb, certain that I'd find something to identify you—a letter, anything. But there wasn't a scrap of paper connected with you.'

'That was Ben's doing,' she said in a daze. 'I remember he insisted on clearing everything out. He was obsessive. I was his property and he wasn't going to leave any trace of me behind with another man.'

'That sounds like Ben. At any rate, there was nothing there. I had to make do with a photograph of you that I found in Angelo's pocket after he died.'

'You gave my photograph to a private eye?' she demanded, aghast.

'It was all I had and, before you condemn me,

you never saw Angelo when they took him out of that car, his face and body smashed…'

'Don't,' she said huskily, turning away so that he couldn't see the tears that sprang to her eyes.

'I felt I was justified in anything I did, so I hired an investigator, but he found nothing. I had to give it up and for years that's where it stood. But last year I heard of another man, called Razzini, practically a genius in this kind of work. He found you in a month.'

'And that was why you offered Ben a job—to get him here, so that he'd bring me,' Elise said bitterly.

'Not just to make him bring you,' Vincente said. 'I hated him on his own account for what he did to Angelo and I wanted to make him pay.'

'How? What were you going to do to him? Bankrupt him? Frame him for a crime and put him in gaol for years?'

'I toyed with the idea. It would have been a pleasure.'

'But you must have decided on something,' she harried him. 'Don't be shy about it at this late date.'

A change was coming over Elise. Deep down she knew there was grief, but she could abandon herself to that later. Anger would be more use to her now.

She stood in front of him, furious and challenging.

'So why don't you give me a blow-by-blow description of everything you've done, starting with that day we met over Ben's grave? I want to know it all—every lie you've told, every deception you've practised. Tell me about the times we've lain together and you've pretended to make love to me with a cheap, cynical laugh in your heart.'

His face darkened in a way that some people would have found frightening, but Elise was too blazingly angry to care.

'How you must have relished that! What did you say to yourself at the time? This one's for Angelo? Or did Angelo's revenge come later— tonight, maybe, when you stood there and watched me as I suddenly saw the truth and understood the whole horrible thing you'd done to me?

'But of course the revenge isn't over, is it? It'll be with me every moment from now on, poisoning each memory I have—not just of you but of him. My God, I was better off with Ben!

'So tell me the whole story. I want to know every last detail, Vincente. Go on. *Tell me!*'

'Shut up and listen,' Vincente snapped. 'If you want me to tell you what my final plans were, I can't. I was waiting to meet you before deciding. Ben boasted about you. He might have betrayed you with every woman he met but he was still

proud to have people know you were his, because
you were beautiful. When I heard the pride in his
voice I knew how I could hurt him.'

'Through me?'

'*Yes.*'

'By doing what? Getting me to betray him,
make a fool of him?'

Vincente didn't answer. Suddenly her eyes
kindled and she struck him. He jerked his head
away but not in time. She could see the mark of
her hand on his face, but he didn't rub it. She
guessed he wouldn't give her the satisfaction.

'That's it, isn't it?' she breathed. 'You'd have put
Ben in the spotlight, made sure the whole world
was looking at him, and then humiliated him as
much as you could. But suppose I wouldn't play
your game? Or were you so certain that I'd fall at
your feet?'

'I'm not as bad as that,' he snapped.

'I think you are. You were sure of me, weren't
you? You thought you couldn't fail, that I was
little better than a hooker who'd follow any man
who dangled money in front of me. That's true,
isn't it? Admit it, damn you!'

'I won't—not the way you put it. Yes, I thought
I had a chance, but you're making it sound worse
than it was.'

'Just how much worse could it get? You have no idea how you sound to an ordinary decent person—that is, if I'm allowed to call myself a decent person, because plainly, in your eyes, I'm not. A bought woman and next thing to a murderess, right?'

'Not now—' he said quickly, and instantly realised his mistake.

'But then. That's how you saw me, isn't it?'

'Before I'd ever met you. All I knew was that Angelo loved you, and you broke his heart.'

'I had no choice but to leave him.'

'I know that now; I didn't know it then.'

'Ah, yes, it's more convenient if you don't know too much. Why burden yourself with accurate facts? Revenge is so much easier when it's blind. You had no idea what really happened, but that didn't stop you judging me, planning to humiliate me as well as Ben.'

Elise waited to see if he would answer this, but he only looked at her out of bleak, haggard eyes.

'So,' she said at last, 'when we were having an affair under the eyes of the whole city—and it would have been the whole city, wouldn't it?— what was going to happen then? Were you going to dump me in public, or wouldn't that have been enough? Was I going to end up in gaol too?'

'Of course not,' he said angrily.

'There's no "of course" about it. You'd have done anything, wouldn't you?'

'Things didn't work out the way I thought. You were different—but Ben was exactly as I expected. I thought I had him—'

Vincente clenched his hand, as though imagining that he had the hapless Ben trapped there.

'And then he died and escaped you,' she said satirically. 'So you had to take it out on me alone. How disappointing for you! Plus you needed to think of another way of getting me here. So you came to Ben's funeral, and took me to dinner that night. I was slipping through your fingers and you had to find a way to hold on to me, didn't you? *Didn't you?*'

'Yes.'

'That's why you tried to persuade me to come back to Rome with you. I wonder what you'd have done if I'd found a buyer for the apartment.'

He didn't answer, and suddenly the truth hit her.

'You did that,' she breathed. 'You fixed it so I couldn't find a buyer. I remember now—there was a man who made an offer but he backed out suddenly. That was your doing.'

'Of course it was. I persuaded him to withdraw his offer…'

'I wonder how you "persuaded" him. Or don't I need to wonder.'

'I was determined to stop you selling this place. It was my only way of getting you to Rome.'

'Oh, I've really got to hand it to you,' she said softly. 'As a shrewd manipulator you're the tops. But of course you have no conscience, which is a big help.'

'*You* lecture me on conscience?'

'I've always had a conscience about Angelo. I treated him badly but I didn't want to. Ben had a hold over me. But you—plotting for eight years without let-up. How could you do that?'

'I saw his dead body,' he shouted. 'I saw what the misery did to my mother. Do you expect me to forget that?'

'Not to forget it, but not to rush to spread blame. You told me not to judge you too easily, but you've judged me every moment for the last eight years. You never thought that there might be something to be said on my side.'

'No, I didn't, and I've blamed myself for that ever since you told me how Ben forced you.'

'But it came too late, didn't it? I was already in the net by then. How you must have enjoyed closing it around me! Every word you said to me was a lie. Even when...'

She checked herself as a wave of anguish washed over her. She fought it with every fibre of her being. She couldn't afford it.

Vincente, watching, drew a tense breath, but stayed still before the rage in her eyes.

'Even when you seemed most sincere, it was a lie,' she said. 'That takes some doing. I congratulate you. It was a good act, but it's over. You served your purpose.'

'And what does that mean?'

'It means you're not the only one concealing their real thoughts. I hadn't slept with a man for years. I was ready for—shall we say?—a new experience. No ties. No conditions. You fitted the bill perfectly.'

That struck home, she was glad to notice. He paled, his mouth tightened and his face had a withered look.

'What are you saying?' he asked warily.

'You know exactly what I'm saying,' Elise said, challenging him with her look. 'I said you were shrewd and calculating, but you're good in another way—just the way I needed. Do you want me to elaborate?'

'I don't think you need to,' he said quietly.

'I didn't know a man could be that skilled in bed,' she went on, disregarding him. 'It's something I won't forget, because it gives me a touch-stone to measure the others by.'

'Others?'

'In the future. And there are going to be others, make no mistake. You did a fine job; now I'm going to discover just how fine. I remember every-thing, you see. Are your special little touches yours alone, or do other men know them? And, if not, how quickly can they be taught? Never mind. I'll have fun finding out.'

'Don't talk like that,' he almost shouted.

'I'll talk as I like. If you don't like it, tough. Remember, I'm partly your creation. I've learned a lot from you, not just about sex but about cruelty and ruthlessness, deception with a straight face. I'm glad of it. Your lessons are going to come in very useful.'

His mouth twisted cynically. 'Well done, Elise. You turned out to be everything I thought of you. I knew you'd show your true colours in the end.'

'Yes, you did, didn't you? And now I have. So have you. So we can toss each other on the scrap heap and go our separate ways without regret.'

'An admirable idea,' he snapped. 'I'm glad you feel you learned something from me.'

'Ruthlessness, manipulation—'

'I'm commonly held to be a master. You've been learning from the best.'

'Every word you ever said to me—'

'Pretence, all of them. Every word, every caress, every moment of passion—all done for a purpose.'

'All those times we made love—?'

'You don't really think I could love you, do you?' he demanded coldly. 'To me, you're little better than a murderess. I know my mother thinks Angelo committed suicide because he couldn't endure what you'd done to him, and perhaps he did—'

'Perhaps?' She seized on this. 'Aren't you sure? Is that what the witnesses said?'

'There were no witnesses. Nobody saw the actual crash.'

'Then it might have been an accident,' she said desperately.

Elise turned away, putting her hands over her ears, but he followed, turning her forcibly, pulling her hands down and holding her.

'Let me go!'

She struggled but his grip on her wrists was vicious.

'No, you're going to listen to me.' He released her hands but imprisoned her again by putting both arms around her and holding her hard against his chest.

'This time you don't get away with blocking it out,' he rasped. 'You're going to hear the truth and live with it, and I hope it destroys you for life, as it's destroyed other people. Are you listening?'

'Yes,' she whispered.

'Angelo had driven that road a hundred times, even in the dark, and never had an accident before. So why that night? Maybe he did it deliberately, or maybe he was so wretched that he didn't notice what he was doing. Either way, it's your doing.'

He stopped, still holding her. His mouth was so close that she could feel his hot breath, as so often in the past when they had embraced. But this time there was only hatred and his desire to hurt her.

She twisted her head away as far as possible so that he couldn't see the tears pouring down her cheeks, but he took her chin, raising it so that he could look into her face, and the tears fell over his hand.

He released her as if stung, and she had to stagger to stop herself falling. Blinded by misery, she didn't see the quick, supportive movement of his hand towards her, a movement that he checked at once.

'I meant to say all this long ago,' he said. 'I should have done, but I weakened for a while because you have your attractions. But, in the end, nothing has really changed. We were always headed for this place.'

She stared at him and forced herself to speak

calmly through the thunder of her heart. 'Nice to get everything clear,' she said.

'Exactly.'

'I want you to leave, Vincente. *Now!*'

He hesitated for a moment and she thought he was about to refuse. But then he made a gesture of resignation and walked out.

When he'd gone Elise stood in the centre of the apartment in a daze, not moving, listening to the silence which seemed to roar in her ears. After a while she began to wander around but not with any purpose, just going here and there without seeing where.

What did you do when your life had crashed into a stone wall?

At last her steps took her to her bedroom where she undressed like an automaton, got into bed and lay staring into the darkness.

Angelo seemed to be there, looking at her with love and reproach. He had loved her, and she'd caused his death. Vincente had been right about that. However it had happened, she had killed him.

'I'm sorry,' she whispered to him. 'I'm so sorry.'

But the reproach was still there in his eyes, and she knew they would haunt her for the rest of her life. The truth would destroy her, as Vincente hoped. And she couldn't even blame him.

Hours passed. Only half realising, she was listening for the phone to ring, but there was only silence.

When morning came she was still awake, still in the same position. She wanted to weep but couldn't. Her heart was frozen.

She managed to get up long enough to splash some water on her face and make some tea. But after one cup she lost interest and returned to bed. She was shivering now and couldn't stop, although the day was warm.

She tried to sleep but there was no escape from the images chasing themselves around her brain in a merciless circle. Angelo had faded now, but there was no relief because his place was taken by Vincente and his deception that had undermined everything, poisoning each memory, leaving her with nothing.

With a sense of horror she recalled their very first meeting, when Vincente had seemed to defend her against Mary by mounting a subtle attack.

'She has a heart of stone and a brain of ice.'

The words had seemed a clever device but now they returned, imbued with a hideous new meaning.

'There's always justice in the end, however long the wait.'

Vincente had sought her out, hating her for what he took to be her heart of stone, looking forward to a 'justice' too long delayed. And his words had been a threat and a warning, if only she could have seen it.

Now there was a hard pain inside her where her heart should have been. It was growing every moment despite her attempts to hold it back. But she was stronger now. She knew the truth, so logically there was no cause for weeping. She would hold on to that thought and make her plans to leave this place, so that she need never see him again.

But the words dissolved into thin air while the pain grew and grew until at last a cry that was almost a scream broke from her, and after that nothing would hold back the sobs.

Elise didn't know how long she wept, but at some point she fell asleep and when she opened her eyes it was light. Tears were still pouring down her cheeks and she wondered if she'd cried as she slept.

'But no more,' she muttered. 'I'll never cry for him again. That's finished. Everything is finished.'

Soon she would get up and resume her normal life. But the minutes passed and she didn't move. She wondered if she would ever move again.

Another day and night passed like this. Distantly she could hear the traffic from the road outside, but there was no other sound. The phone never rang. She felt dead. Her heart was dead, her body was dead. Only her brain lived and it was full of scorn for herself and how easily she'd been deluded.

The signs had been there from the start. On the first evening she'd even jokingly accused him of coming for revenge, and his startled reaction should have warned her that something was amiss. But she'd been too deluded by her attraction to him to heed the signs.

And when he'd returned, months later, she'd told herself that he was as attracted to her as she to him—that was why he couldn't stay away.

Fool! Idiot!

From outside she could hear the rain begin, growing louder as it turned into a thunderstorm. She could hear the water pounding against the window and it seemed to blend with her tears, which wouldn't stop. She fell asleep again, but the storm pursued her so that the thunder and lightning became part of her own grief. When she awoke she had the feeling that she'd slept the clock round, perhaps twice. She no longer knew anything.

At last she managed to stand up and make her way to the kitchen, where she poured herself some mineral water, but suddenly she become nauseous and ran for the bathroom.

After so long without food, all she could do was heave helplessly, but at last it stopped and she managed to get back to the kitchen and make some tea. The hot liquid soothed her insides, giving her a brief rush of energy.

She needed to get out of this echoing place where his malign ghost seemed to mock her. Anywhere would do. Another cup of hot tea strengthened her enough for her to dress and leave the building. She found that it was later than she'd thought, with the light already fading as she made her way along the street.

Elise was vaguely aware that people were looking at her but she didn't care. Lights swirled about her, traffic roared in her ears, but she had only one thought. She must get to the Trevi Fountain. Angelo was waiting for her there, and there was something she must say to him. He'd waited too long to hear it, and if she delayed he might be gone and never hear the words—if only she could remember what they were.

She quickened her pace, turning across the road in the direction she was sure led to the fountain. But halfway across she became confused. A huge truck was bearing down on her. There were shouts and screaming from the side of the road, and the next moment she was lying unconscious on the ground.

CHAPTER NINE

FOR four days Vincente's staff had been regarding him nervously. He arrived early, stayed late and worked with a face like thunder. He spoke briefly, seemed impatient of company and seemed abnormally conscious of the telephone.

The only person he trusted was his secretary, well briefed on the calls to be blocked and those to be put through. One call, she knew, never came.

Vincente was set on being patient. She would call him. He was certain of that. Too much was left unresolved between them, and she had no choice but to call.

He had only one thing to cling to, and that was the fact that he'd managed to hide his true feelings. His shock and confusion at the first sight of her in his mother's home must have been visible, but after that he was sure he'd kept his defences in place.

His plan to track her down for revenge had begun to go wrong on the day he'd met her. She'd been so different from the cheap floozy of his expectations that he'd been disconcerted, fascinated. When she'd rejected him that evening he'd known frustration but also satisfaction that she couldn't be so easily seduced.

Through the months apart he'd worked to stop the sale of her apartment, determined to lure her to Rome. He'd told himself it was because his revenge must be achieved, refusing to face the true reason—that he'd met the one woman he couldn't forget, who physically enticed him without boring him even for a moment.

There had been too many women in his life. They hurled themselves at his money and his looks, and laid themselves out to please him. But Elise challenged him, fought with him, cheerfully insulted him, and he always went back for more. Not for Angelo's sake. For his own.

Since she'd come to Rome he'd thought of little else but being with her, when he would see her again, the feeling of having her in his bed. At times he'd almost forgotten about Angelo, and the things he needed to know. It was always there, but less important than the shine of her eyes, the feel of her body against his and the cry of fulfilment in the dark that mingled with his own.

But what really stood out in his mind wasn't

their sexual encounters, sweet though they were. It was the time sex had been denied them, when he'd lain in her bed for days, almost helpless, reliant on her assistance. And in the long nights they had talked, coming close to understanding each other.

No, honesty checked him. His deception had denied her any understanding of him. It was he who had got to know her, and learned that he'd misjudged her.

The turning point had come when she'd told him how Ben had forced her hand. It meant that she was innocent, he could think well of her, and this had caused a leap of joy in his heart that warned him where his feelings were heading. Looking back to those days and nights now, he knew it had been the best time of his life.

But he'd found himself trapped. The longer they were together, the more his plans for revenge had seemed like nonsense. Somehow he would find a way out of the mess, tell her the truth and clear the air between them, but without revealing the extent of his plotting. He'd never doubted that he would be able to do this. He'd always been able to do anything that he set his mind to.

But then she'd discovered everything in the worst possible way, forcing him to see that he was lost in a labyrinth of his own making. Taken by surprise, he'd hesitated, briefly unsure how to confront her.

But then she'd attacked him with scorn, jeering at him as a lover, and he'd snapped, turning on her, returning cruelty for cruelty. Inwardly he groaned to recall how he'd laid all the blame for Angelo's death on her, when the truth was that she, as much as Angelo, had been Ben's victim. He'd known that, yet still he'd hurled it at her with a savage satisfaction that shamed him now.

Why the hell didn't she call him?

For him to call her was impossible. She would gain the upper hand—something he couldn't afford.

Unless the call was strictly business.

It would make sense to let her know that he would no longer block the sale of her apartment, so that she could sell up and leave. That would show her that he was unrelenting, while still allowing him to hear her voice.

'I don't want to be disturbed until I call you,' Vincente told his secretary.

When he was alone he dialled her cellphone but it was switched off. He tried her apartment but there was no reply.

After half an hour he called again, but couldn't get through on either phone. At his secretary's in-

sistence he accepted an urgent business call but
dealt with it only from the top of his head. Then
he tried once more. But there was nothing.

After so long this might mean anything; she
might have left the country.

'Hold all my calls,' he said, rising abruptly. 'I'll
be out for the rest of the day.'

'But you have a meeting with a government
minister—'

'Cancel it.' He was halfway out of the door.

Twenty minutes later he reached her apartment
and rang the bell impatiently, planning what he
would say when he saw her, but there was no
response. Suddenly filled with dread, he pressed
hard on the bell, keeping his finger there.

'You're wasting your time,' said a woman's voice
from further along the corridor. 'She isn't there.'

'Do you know where she is?'

'In hospital, since yesterday. She was knocked
down in the street, by a truck.'

The elderly doctor looked up at the man who came
racing down the corridor as though all the devils
in hell were after him.

'I'm here to see Signora Carlton.'

'Are you a relative, *signore*?'

'No, does it matter?'

'I mean, you are not her husband?'

'Her husband is dead. My name is Vincente Farnese.'

Most people reacted to that name—impressed or even scared. The doctor seemed barely to have heard it.

'I see. She hasn't been able to speak much, you understand. She drifts in and out of consciousness.'

'Dear God!' Vincente whispered. 'What did that truck do to her?'

'Nothing, *signore*. It didn't hit her. She merely collapsed in the road in front of it. Luckily the driver had sharp reactions and braked in time to avoid her.'

'Collapsed? What do you mean?'

'She seems to be suffering some severe trauma, apart from not having eaten anything for days.'

Vincente closed his eyes. But the doctor's next words made him open them sharply.

'We're doing our best to save the baby, but I must warn you that nothing is certain.'

'A baby?' he whispered.

'You didn't know, *signore*?'

'I had no idea.'

'Well, it's very early days. She didn't know about it herself until I told her. But I'm afraid that it may already be too late.'

'I want to see her,' Vincente demanded.

'I'm not sure that will be possible.'

'What do you mean, not possible?' he snapped. 'That's my child she's carrying—'

'But you're not her husband. There are rules about these things. I can't let you in without her consent.'

Vincente was about to lose his temper in the way that had served him so well before with people who needed to be shown who was boss, but mercifully something stopped him.

'Please ask her,' he said quietly. Then, as the doctor turned away, he stopped him. 'Doctor— beg her if you have to.'

The doctor nodded in understanding and disappeared. Alone, Vincente turned away to look out of the window. He cared nothing for the view but he didn't want anyone to see his face, lest it reflect the feelings that were tearing him apart.

For once a situation was completely beyond his control. Something ancient and fundamental in him had leapt at the discovery that he was to be a father. Not for a moment did he doubt that Elise's child was his. Now he had to face the fact that she could refuse to see him, could lose their baby without his being there, could even deny his paternity, if her hatred of him was great enough.

And why shouldn't she hate him? He'd tricked

her, always holding part of himself aloof behind the barrier of his deception. She'd captivated and confused him, so that his whole relationship with her had been coloured by that confusion, and there had been in him a dishonesty that had justified the contempt he'd seen in her eyes.

Now she might view him with even more contempt if his behaviour had damaged her enough to destroy their child.

For once in his life he was helpless, and he wanted to howl his despair and frustration.

He turned quickly as the doctor reappeared.

'Will she see me?' he asked sharply.

'She did not refuse,' the doctor said cautiously. 'In fact she said nothing.' His eyes were suddenly kinder. 'I think I'm justified in taking silence as consent.'

Vincente followed him along two corridors, shocked to discover that he was frightened. He had no idea how to face her, what to say to her.

In the event his fears were wasted. When the doctor finally led him into a corner room a nurse rose, saying, 'She fell asleep again as soon as you left, Doctor.'

'What are those things she's attached to?' Vincente demanded.

'This one is a blood transfusion,' the doctor explained, 'and the other is a saline drip. They'll help to keep her strength up.'

'And the baby?'

He checked the machines. 'The signs are good.'

'Let me stay with her,' Vincente said. 'I'll call if anything happens.'

'All right, but let her sleep while she needs to.'

When they had gone Vincente sat down beside the bed, his eyes fixed on Elise. Had she really fallen asleep, or was she merely pretending, in order to avoid him?

Gently he touch her hand with the back of his fingers. She didn't flinch away as he'd dreaded, and that told him that she really was unconscious.

He wondered at himself. She had said things to him, torturing him for her own satisfaction in a way that should make him hate her, except that he knew she'd been acting out of self-defence. That was how she saw him now—as a threat to be faced down. And it was all his own fault.

She stirred and muttered, twisting her head on the pillow so that he gained a clearer view of her face. He thought she would open her eyes, but she didn't. Moving very gently, he ventured to take her hand, carefully avoiding all the tubes to which she was attached.

'Elise,' he murmured, 'I'm here.'

A terrible stillness fell over her, as though this was the worst thing that he could have said. She wanted nothing to do with him. She'd made that very plain.

'Can you hear me?' he asked gently.

'Yes.' Her whisper seemed to come from a great distance.

'I came as soon as I heard what happened to you.'

Silence. He couldn't tell if she was still with him.

'I wanted to say I was sorry,' he said, leaning closer to her. 'I said terrible things that I didn't mean. Elise—please believe that I'm sorry.'

Then she opened her eyes, but his heart sank as he saw no yielding in them.

'Sorry,' she echoed. 'I said I was sorry…to Angelo…the day after I arrived here. I went to the Trevi Fountain…we were there together once. I threw in a coin and made a wish that I'd come back to Rome…and I did, didn't I?'

He dropped his head into his hands.

'I wanted to be with him for ever…but then he died. I didn't know he'd died like that, and it was my fault…'

'It wasn't,' he groaned.

'It was. I wrote to him when I got back to England, telling him what had happened, that I still loved him and always would. I could never forget how he stood under the window, screaming as he saw me in Ben's arms. I thought if he knew the truth—that I hadn't really betrayed him—he could endure it better.'

'I don't think it ever arrived,' Vincente said.

'Of course not. I found it among Ben's things after he died. I don't know how he stole it, but he managed somehow. But if Angelo died that same night…'

'He wouldn't have got it.'

'So he never knew that I was sorry, that I always loved him and didn't betray him in my heart. He'll never know that.'

Elise fell silent, as though speaking had exhausted her.

'The doctor tells me that we're going to have a child,' he said at last.

She looked at him. 'We?'

'You're pregnant. He says he told you.'

'Yes—but I thought it was just a bad dream.'

He shook his head, unable to speak.

If only, Vincente thought, she would say something else. Surely she understood that this made a difference.

'I'm glad about it,' he said at last, 'if you are.'

She made no reply.

'I think we should marry as soon as possible,' he persisted.

She stared at him as though he was insane.

'Us? Marry?' She began to shake with feeble laughter.

'For pity's sake, don't do that,' he said harshly.

'Oh, heavens! And I thought you didn't have a sense of humour. *Marry.*'

'We could put the past behind us—'

'You can never put the past behind you. I know that now, and so should you. The only way we'll ever know peace is apart. And peace is all I care about. It feels like the most important thing in the world.'

'More important than love?'

Then he wished he hadn't said that, because she gave him a look of such bitter scorn that his heart nearly shrivelled inside him.

'You know nothing of love,' she said huskily. 'You only know about acquiring things and making people dance to your tune. Whatever you want, you must have, including revenge. Someone should have stood up to you long ago.'

'But you did,' he reminded her. 'You're the only person who didn't do what I wanted.'

'And I never will. Go away. Leave now and don't come back.'

'I can't leave you and our child.'

'I don't ever want to see you again. It's nothing to you whether I have a child or not.'

'Don't do this.'

She was going to reply but suddenly everything became foggy. His face came and went in her consciousness, leaving only his horrified expression and the appalled note in his voice as he called for help.

Then the room was full of people, connecting her to new apparatus, checking, taking readings, talking to each other in urgent voices. Fear seized her as she thought of her baby. Whatever she'd told him, she couldn't bear to lose it.

She could just make him out, several feet away by the window. He should be here with her, giving her strength to save their child. But it was she who'd set him at a distance, and now he could only stand there and watch as she lost the baby and the last link between them was cut.

When Elise opened her eyes it was night and Vincente was in the same position by the window, as though held frozen by a curse.

'Is it over?' she asked hoarsely.

At last he came closer and sat by the bed, straining to hear her.

'The baby—it's gone?'

'No,' he said at once. 'They gave you another blood transfusion and things started to get better. Our baby's alive, and it's going to stay that way. From now on I'm going to look after you and make sure you're both all right. Don't argue with me. We're going to be married, and that's final.'

'All right.' The words were little more than a breath, so soft that he wasn't sure that he'd heard her.

'Our child will be born in wedlock,' he said gently.

'Yes—of course.'

Had any man ever received such joyless consent? It was as though she accepted him in despair—with no hope, only resignation.

He wasn't an imaginative man, but for a moment he was granted a glimpse of the future—a bleak road stretching far into the distance, with the two of them trudging endlessly together towards nothing. And he was appalled.

The thing that shocked him most was her agreement with whatever he suggested. She, who had always stood up to him, teased and fenced with him, who had only a few hours ago told him to go to hell, now agreed without argument to whatever he said.

He had always been a dominant man, demanding exactly this kind of acquiescence as of right. But from her he hated it.

Even so, he seized the chance to make his other demand while she was in this mood. It was too important for him to take risks.

'The doctor says you can leave soon,' he said, 'and I want to take you home with me.'

'Home?'

'The Palazzo Marini. You mustn't live alone. It's too dangerous for you.'

'You expect me to live—*there*?'

He knew what she meant. There, where she had discovered his deception and the world had exploded around her.

'No,' she said angrily. 'I just want to go home and be alone.'

'That I won't allow,' he said flatly, and caught himself up at once. 'I mean—it would be better to do it my way.'

'No, no, you got it right the first time,' she said with weary irony. 'Stick to giving orders. It's what you do best, and at least then we all know how things really stand, which is very useful. I like knowing the truth.'

Her soft bitterness shocked him and made him clench his hands out of sight.

'Elise—' he whispered.

'I can't live with your mother. How would she bear looking at me every day, knowing that I was the woman who destroyed Angelo?'

'She knows nothing. We didn't quarrel in front of her that night, and I never spoke a word about it afterwards.'

She gave a hard, mirthless laugh that tore at his

heart. 'Of course, how much easier to deceive her! Why didn't I think of that?'

'She's had a lot of pain in her life. Angelo's death hit her hard, and I don't tell her anything that might upset her.'

She gave a faint, derisive smile. 'And you're going to take the risk of leaving me alone with her? Suppose I tell her?'

'You won't do that. It would be cruel and spiteful, and you're not either of those things.'

'I thought we'd established that I was.'

'You told me what Ben did—'

'How do you know I was telling the truth—such a deceiver as I am?'

'Stop it,' he growled.

'But we must be realistic, mustn't we?' she challenged with a touch a grim humour that came strangely from her weakened frame. 'Think how good I must be at thinking up the right lies.'

'I forbid you to talk like that,' he said fiercely.

At once she closed her eyes, seeming to sag wearily as though she could only fight just so much.

'All right,' she whispered. 'Believe what you like.'

'You forget, I got to know Ben. It's easy to believe he'd behave like that.'

She opened her eyes again. 'Yes, you knew Ben. At one time I thought you knew me—'

This time she turned her head right away from him, and he could say no more.

Would it always be there between them? Vincente wondered. He'd learned to think the best of her, but would she ever forget or forgive the fact that it had needed to be learned?

As soon as Elise was stronger Vincente brought his mother to see her. Signora Farnese was almost weeping with joy at the thought of the coming wedding and her first grandchild.

Elise could see how frail this woman was. Vincente had been born late in her life and she was in her seventies. She had known little happiness, and was eager to grasp what was left.

'I knew this was going to happen,' she said cheerily. 'When I first saw the two of you together, I knew everything. There was a special "something" between you that only happens between people in love.'

Vincente and Elise could not meet each other's eyes. Luckily his mother was oblivious.

A few days later she was installed in the Palazzo Marini, in the grand bedroom that was exclusive to the mistress of the house. The huge bed was hung with brocade curtains that swept up to a point over the pillows, where they were topped by something that looked suspiciously like a coronet.

The bedroom was only for Elise. Vincente's room was even more grandiose. They were connected by a short, narrow corridor, little more than a cupboard, which also contained the entrance to their bathroom.

'Perfectly horrible,' the *Signora* said. 'I always hated this suite, and Vincente has always slept in a small room on the other side of the house. But of course you will both have to move in here or the Marini ghosts will disapprove.'

She set about spoiling Elise very thoroughly, insisting that she should call her Mamma. Elise agreed, finding solace in the older woman's kindness.

She felt stranded in no man's land. She had wanted to separate from Vincente, and only the threatened loss of her baby had made her change her mind. Then a powerful surge of maternal feeling had made her determined to give the child everything it deserved, including a father. She had agreed to the marriage because in her mind all other paths had closed off.

But where did that leave the two of them? She had yet to find out.

The ceremony was to take place at the Church of Santa Navona, a magnificent edifice where the family had always been married and buried.

'Does that mean Angelo's there?' Elise asked Vincente.

'Yes. Do you want me to show you the place?'

'No need. Just tell me where it is.'

'If you don't mind, I'd rather take you myself.'

She did mind, he could see that at once. She wanted to be alone with Angelo, but a fierce jealousy that he would not admit to made Vincente insist on going too. For a moment he thought she might argue, but then she shrugged as though it really didn't matter very much, because nothing mattered any more. And that hurt him more than anything.

'Before we go to the grave,' he said, 'I've got something to tell you. The night you told me about Angelo, you said his name was Caroni. That threw me, because it wasn't. It was Valetti. Caroni was his mother's maiden name.'

'But why—?'

'I suppose using it was part of his assertion of independence, the illusion of being a poor student who had to live in Trastevere.'

When they reached the churchyard he led her to the grave, which was under the trees, just visible from the path that led to the front door. A length of marble lay flat on the ground, with the name Angelo Valetti engraved in it, and his dates.

'So even he didn't tell me the complete truth,' she mused. 'Can any of you be trusted?'

'Don't judge him too harshly. It was a game to him.'

'That's why I couldn't find any trace of his death,' she breathed. 'I tried to check his death certificate as soon as I arrived. I wanted to know how and why he'd died. But of course there was nobody of that name. Will you leave me, please? I'd like to be alone with Angelo.'

Reluctantly he walked away.

Elise looked a long time at the date of Angelo's death, which was the same as the day he'd stood under her window and cried out his despair at the sight of her in Ben's arms. She'd known it in her head, yet seeing it written like this brought a sharp reality that was almost unbearable.

Then she looked at where Angelo's photograph had been imprinted in the marble and drew a long, tremulous breath, fighting the despair that threatened to engulf her. The picture showed a young man smiling with the joy of life. His love and eagerness glowed from him.

Once he had been hers.

She dropped to her knees so that she could run her fingertips over his face as she'd done so many times before. Except for her own water colour, this was the first time she'd seen his face for years.

'Even you weren't what you said,' she whispered. 'I thought I'd find you again in Rome but you've been hiding from me all the time. Nothing but lies and illusions.'

But this mood couldn't last. His deception had been innocent enough next to Vincente's, and now he was dead.

'I'm sorry,' she whispered. 'I never knew...I tried to tell you...I wrote but you never saw it. If only you were here so that I could talk to you. I didn't want to be Ben's wife, or Vincente's. You were the one I wanted to marry. But now...'

She laid her hand over her stomach.

Vincente, watching her from a distance, saw everything he didn't want to see. She was pleading with Angelo, no doubt begging his forgiveness because she was carrying Vincente's child, telling him that she wished it was his.

He turned away and the taste in his mouth was very bitter.

At last she returned and he drove her home in silence.

CHAPTER TEN

THE wedding was the quietest possible, taking place in a little side chapel of the great church. There was no grand bridal gown or bridesmaids similarly attired, no church packed with business associates passing as friends, no thunderous organ music, no procession down the aisle and back, no press interest.

Instead, with the bare minimum of witnesses, two people who were secretly afraid of each other, and of themselves, pledged mutual love and honour for the rest of their lives.

To please his mother, Vincente began their wedding night in Elise's room.

'Give her time to retire for the night, then I'll go away and leave you in peace,' he said.

'Thank you.'

'Are you feeling all right? You looked very pale during the service.'

'I'm fine. I got over my bad spell at the beginning. The doctor says I'm strong again—strong enough to give birth to a Farnese son or daughter.'

'I was concerned for you, for your own sake, not just as the mother of my child. But I suppose you don't believe that.'

'No, I believe whatever you tell me.'

Her voice was calm, emotionless, and he wanted to shout at her to look at him, respond to him—anything to awaken her from the chilly trance into which she had retreated. Horrified, he realised that anything he did would only drive her further into hiding. She'd found a place where he couldn't reach her.

From the corridor outside they heard the sound of footsteps, followed by Mamma's voice. 'Goodnight, both of you. It's all right, I'm not coming in.'

'Thank you, Mamma,' Vincente called in a strained voice. 'Goodnight.'

If they had been uneasy before, the old lady's heavy-handed tact made it a hundred times worse. It was clear that she was enjoying a fantasy in which the bride and groom stripped seductively, prior to making passionate love, not watching each other from each side of a yawning distance.

Elise turned away to the tall window and looked down into the garden where the servants were having an impromptu party.

'They're celebrating,' she murmured.

Vincente came up behind her.

'Of course. A wedding is always good news for a family even if...well.'

A yell of delight reached them from below. Some of the party-goers looked up to the window and raised their glasses in salute, laughing and cheering.

'They can see us,' he said, pushing the window so that it opened on to a small balcony. 'It's you they want.'

Taking her hand, he drew her out and a riot of good cheer soared up to greet them. Glasses were raised, greetings and congratulations were shouted. Elise could just make out the words *la signora* and *bambino*.

'I suppose everyone knows,' she said.

'No, but they suspect and they're hoping.'

She summoned up a smile, waving at the little crowd below, and they responded with a shout of joy. One middle-aged man called up daringly, *'Bambino? Si?'*

Elise put her hands over her stomach, smiled and nodded, which produced an explosion of cheering. Vincente too was smiling as he moved a little closer, laying a hand on her shoulder, close to her neck.

'Look at me,' he murmured.

As she did so he delighted their audience further

by laying his mouth on hers. She accepted the kiss and leaned into it, prepared to seem willing because it was only part of the performance.

Elise thought she was braced for the feel of his lips, but then he did something unfair. Either by accident or design, his hand moved to the back of her neck, caressing exactly the spot he'd discovered when she'd last lain in his arms, the night he'd cynically inflamed her desire as a way to show her who was boss.

The result was the same now as then. Despite her mind's resistance, a flash of lightning seemed to go through her, threatening all her resolutions.

Did he know? Of course he did, she thought bitterly. This man did nothing without calculating the consequences down to the last detail.

He put his hand on the other side of her face so that what appeared to the onlookers below was not a passionate kiss, but one full of tender consideration. Cheers rose to engulf them.

'I think we should go in now,' she whispered.

Nodding, he waved to the crowd and they went back inside.

'They love you,' Vincente said warmly. 'You did everything right. Thank you.'

'Don't thank me,' she said coolly. 'I'm an old hand at this. Years with Ben taught me how to hide hostility with a smile.'

He was standing close, not touching her, but looking searchingly into her face.

'Hostility?' he echoed. 'To them?'

'Not to them.'

'Elise—'

'What did you expect? Have you forgotten the last time we met before you went away? You set out that night to show me who called the shots. And you did. You made it very plain who was boss and I got the message. Congratulations. Now you've got your wife and child safely secured under your roof, and all's right with your world.

'But listen to me, Vincente. Don't ever think I'm just going to lie down for you to walk over me. Push me too hard and you'll find that there are limits to your power.'

'Perhaps power isn't all I want.'

'I'm afraid it's all you have. But don't worry, I won't show you up. I'll smile and parade and be nice to the right people. As I said, I got lots of practise with Ben.'

'I'm not Ben,' he shouted.

'I used to think you weren't,' she said softly. 'But I guess I'm not as good a judge of character as I thought. You'd better go now.'

He looked at her for a long moment. Then he walked out.

* * *

Elise guessed it wasn't coincidence that he was away for the next few days. She was grateful to him for his tact. It gave her time to come to terms with her confusion. Lying alone in the silence of the night, she finally admitted that she had fallen in love with him. She wasn't sure when, but it was some time ago, and too late now. She'd denied it to herself, but now there could be no more denial.

She had given her heart to a man who'd hated and despised her from the first moment, who'd pursued her with the fixed intention of destroying and humiliating her, and who had done it very thoroughly.

In fact, she thought wretchedly, he had no idea just how successful he'd been. At all costs he mustn't realise that she'd been foolish enough to love him, because that would be his final revenge, the most bitter one of all.

But killing her love should be easy. She just had to be strong-minded about it and remember what he'd done. It would take time, but she would work at it. She could be as strong-minded as he.

And he would help deaden her feelings, for there was no reason to expect now that he would be faithful. No doubt from now on he would be spending more time in his bachelor flat, on the pretext of catching up with work.

But there she was wrong. Although he was sometimes late returning to the Palazzo, he never stayed away overnight unless he had to. His manner towards herself was always solicitous and concerned, just as it was to his mother, whose health was frail.

To Elise's relief, her own health and strength returned swiftly. She began to feel equal to anything, even the party that was being planned to celebrate the wedding.

'The whole of Rome is longing to see you,' Mamma told her ecstatically.

'Surely not.' Elise laughed.

'The whole of Rome might be an exaggeration,' Vincente admitted, 'but you've aroused much interest among my friends and associates.'

He gave her a couple of names. One, he had to explain, was the chairman of Italy's most important bank, but she recognised the other.

'Attilo Vansini?' she echoed, stunned. 'But he's…'

He was a figure of enormous political power, always close to the president of the country, whoever the president happened to be. Elections came and went but Vansini maintained his influence, through a combination of wealth, shrewd dealings and corruption, so it was said.

Scandal followed him as dogs followed a scent: women, money, he welcomed it all.

'He said not to forget to invite him to the party,' Vincente told her. 'At that stage I hadn't thought about a party, so this is his way of saying he expects one.'

'You must have a gown made for you by Menotti,' Mamma said, naming the most exclusive couturier in Rome.

Elise would have liked to design her own gown, but realised that it was probably a little soon for that and allowed herself to be swept off to the Via dei Condotti. There they entered a tiny establishment, so unpretentious that it almost seemed to be cowed by the rest of the expensive street.

But inside everything was different. Luisa Menotti was the best, and everything in her salon whispered discreet, luxurious elegance. She took personal charge, exclaiming over Elise's still-slim figure, admiring her fair colouring, and pronouncing, 'Black. Nothing else will do.'

Since Elise had made the same decision, it was a successful visit. The gown that resulted was black silk, low-cut, but no more than modesty allowed, fitting snugly over her hips and sweeping the floor.

She had often entertained lavishly for Ben and was prepared to play a part in the preparations of the Palazzo, but she soon realised that the best thing she could do was to keep out until she understood the Palazzo better.

A hundred in-house servants were mobilised, a hundred more brought in from the Farnese estate in the country. Every inch of the building was cleaned. The extensive grounds were trimmed and prepared, for the party would spill out into the open. Fairy lights hung from the trees, leading far into the distance, creating a mysterious, glowing path.

The Palazzo boasted three kitchens, only one of which was normally used. But during the last two days before the party all three were hard at work.

Deliveries were made from nearby shops so that every guest would have a gift. Elise gasped as she realised what some of them must have cost. Could Vincente really afford all this?

'Why not?' he asked with a shrug when she mentioned it.

They were in the office that he used when working at home, and he had to look up from his desk.

'Well, I know it's important to impress people,' she said. 'Ben used to—'

'Forget Ben. This is a different universe from the one where he operated.'

'Only in the sense that it's bigger,' she retorted. 'When we walk out there together you'll be showing off your trophy in exactly the same way that he did. And I'll walk down those marble steps very slowly and carefully, so that everyone gets a good look at your latest purchase, and tries to calculate whether you were cheated.'

'They can think what they like. If I've been cheated I'll know for myself, without asking anyone else's opinion.'

'And what's your opinion so far?' she challenged. 'Am I worth it?'

He thrust back his chair, rising sharply to his feet and looking her up and down with cool eyes. 'Not yet,' he said at last. 'But I intend that you shall be.'

She gasped. 'Of all the—'

'You started this conversation. If this is how you wish to regard our marriage, then fine, I'll go along with it. I'll give you an accounting now and then to let you know if your value has gone up. If it's gone down I'll tell you why and expect you to put matters right without delay. Anything less would make a fool of me in front of people whose respect I need, and that I won't tolerate. Am I making myself clear?'

'You bastard,' she whispered.

'It was your choice, so we'll play it your way. I want the best from you, especially when I show off my acquisition to an admiring audience.'

'Yes, we wouldn't want them to think you were losing your grip,' she said satirically.

'Exactly; I'm glad you understand. So this would be a good moment to make sure you're properly arrayed. Mamma says your gown is excellent, so all you need now is appropriate jewellery.'

'I'll go shopping tomorrow.'

'No need, I have it here.'

Vincente turned to a well-armoured safe, keyed in the combination and took out several boxes, which he laid on the desk and opened.

Elise's eyes opened wide as the sight of the most magnificent diamonds she had ever seen. There was a fabulous tiara, a large riviere to go about her neck, a heavy bracelet, long ear drops. Each stone was dazzling in its beauty. The effect of them all together was awesome.

'I hope you feel these make a suitable wedding gift,' Vincente said smoothly. 'I'd have given them earlier but they were only delivered today. Turn around.'

Elise did so and he took up the riviere and draped it around her neck. His fingers brushed her gently as he fastened it, and she braced herself against the pleasure of being touched exactly there. Vincente seemed oblivious, which was almost as much of a relief as it was annoying.

'I chose well,' he said. 'They suit you perfectly.'

'But when did you choose them?'

'Last week. I told the shop what I wanted and they did a good job.'

'*You* told the shop? Suppose I had an opinion?'

'Are you saying you don't like them?'

'No, they're beautiful, but I would have liked a say in the choice.'

'I know what suits your style, and I know what my wife will be expected to wear on such an occasion. You look magnificent. You'll be a credit to me.'

A credit to him, she noted. There was no hint of giving pleasure to her.

'You'd better leave them here,' Vincente said. 'I'll put them in the safe until then. Afterwards they can go to the bank—all except this.'

He'd taken her left hand and was putting a ring on the wedding finger, saying, 'It's your engagement ring. You can't appear without one.'

'Did you offer it to me on bended knee?' she asked ironically.

He matched her, irony for irony. 'I'm afraid I can't remember.'

'I don't want them,' she said suddenly.

'What did you say?'

'I don't want these. You talk about a wedding gift, but it's a business transaction, no more.'

'There's nothing wrong with a business transaction as long as it's honest.'

She met his eyes. 'Are we honest? Were we ever?' She began to remove the diamonds.

'Be careful,' he snapped, brushing her hands aside and taking over. 'They're valuable. Do you want to break them?'

'Valuable things get broken all the time, Vincente. We both know that, don't we?'

He grimaced. 'You're right, of course. How could I have forgotten?'

At last the jewels were off and he replaced them in the safe.

'Best if you return them to the jeweller,' she said. 'I shan't wear them.'

He turned on her. 'You will wear them because they are appropriate to *my wife*, and I will allow nothing else. Is that clear?'

She gave a cruel laugh. 'Perfectly clear. Ben himself couldn't have said it any clearer.'

She stormed out, leaving Vincente to fight the temptation to thump the wall. That scene should have gone differently, with him making her a gift of diamonds and her perhaps even being a little pleased. Instead, she'd managed to drive him to the edge of his temper and he'd turned on her, hurling the gift at her contemptuously, thus justifying her worst thoughts about him.

Was that what she wanted? Did it give her a perverse pleasure to provoke his ugly side? He had a terrible feeling that this was exactly the truth.

As she showered and dressed Elise could hear the orchestra already beginning to play in the great ballroom where the party was to be held. Her hair was swept up in a style of elegant sophistication and her make-up was discreetly provocative.

She had changed, she thought. The woman who'd arrived in Rome months ago had considered herself experienced, but there had still been something unawakened about her. In retrospect she could see that. Regarding her reflection in the mirror now, she was struck by the difference. The face that looked back had learned many lessons—some ecstatic, some bitter. Good and bad, they would stay with her for ever.

There was a knock on her door.

'Come in,' she called.

Vincente entered, wearing evening attire and looking so handsome that she had to close her eyes in resistance.

'I've brought your diamonds,' he said.

'Fine,' she told him, smiling. 'Please put them on for me but, before you do, can you zip up my dress?'

She turned her back to him, glancing over her

shoulder so that she could catch his startled reaction to what he saw. The zip was a long one, reaching halfway down the swell of her hips and leaving no doubt about one thing.

'You're not wearing anything under that dress,' Vincente said in a tense voice.

'I can't risk any lines underneath. You wouldn't want me to look unsophisticated, would you?'

'I'd want you to look decent,' he snapped.

'I will. Once you've zipped me up, nobody will see anything. The bust has support built in, so I'll be entirely proper.'

'That's not the word I'd use.'

'Just zip me up, please. People will be arriving soon.'

As though bored by the conversation, she turned her back on him completely, giving him a perfect view of silky skin. Scowling, he drew the zip up so that she was gradually enclosed. As she had said, from the outside her nakedness was impossible to detect.

But it was equally impossible to forget. It was there before his mind's eye as he fastened the tiara, the earrings, the bracelet, the engagement ring and the necklace. When he'd done that, he rested his hands on her bare shoulders and their eyes met in the mirror.

She smiled, and it contained a message. She was letting him know that she could follow his thoughts right back to the first night they'd met. That night too, she'd worn nothing beneath her dress and he'd known, and later had accused her of inciting him deliberately. Which was true. The evening had been full of promise and excitement.

Now she was repeating the trick with the skill of a conjurer, but this time to underline how much had changed. No promise, no excitement, no hope. Only a blazing cynicism tormenting him with the reminder of what was over.

'Satisfied?' she asked lightly. 'Will I do you credit? Will everyone look at me and know how much I cost?'

'They'll know I acquired the best,' he agreed.

'The best and most expensive. Don't forget what really matters.'

'Don't talk like that.'

'But surely you can pay me a compliment on how much my share value has risen tonight? Or will you wait until the end of the evening when you can judge the effect I've had?'

'*Stop it!*' he said explosively, while his hands tightened on her shoulders.

'Be careful; you'll leave bruises,' she said, and he released her at once.

'Let us at least try to seem amicable tonight,' he suggested tensely.

'Of course. You can rely on me to play my role to perfection.'

'Then there's no more to be said. Let's go.'

As they walked towards the ballroom Elise caught a glimpse of them in a full-length mirror and thought how ironic it was that they made such a splendid, well-suited couple. Her appearance was dazzling, the diamonds and black silk setting each other off to perfection. And if there was a more handsome man in the room than Vincente, she would be surprised.

Their entrance into the ballroom was made down a flight of shallow marble steps. At the sight of them the crowd below burst into applause. Vincente drew her arm through his and, heads up, they walked down together.

There were nearly seven hundred guests, some of whom Elise had read about beforehand so that she was able to greet them knowledgeably. From the start instinct told her that she was making a good impression. The men gazed at her with frank appreciation, the women regarded her with envy, though whether they were eyeing her beauty, her diamonds or her husband she couldn't be quite certain. She guessed a mixture of all three.

Secretly, she had to admit that she was glad of her jewels. They were costlier and more glamorous than those of any other woman there, and they marked her out as special.

There was an impressive number of government ministers present, also several film stars. One in particular—a young woman in her twenties who had just scored her first big success in Hollywood—gave Vincente a significant smile that made Elise wonder about their past.

Mentally she shrugged. What was it to her?

Attilo Vansini fulfilled all her expectations, being in his sixties with an unconvincing head of red hair, and an air of bonhomie that was almost violent. He kissed her hand repeatedly, paid a dozen compliments to her looks and demanded that she dance with him first.

'But not before me,' Vincente said, sliding his arm possessively around Elise's waist. 'After all, this is my bride.'

Vansini gave a riotous laugh. 'I defer to love.'

Everyone applauded as the music struck up and the bridal couple began to dance, circling the floor alone.

'He defers to love,' Vincente said. 'In their eyes we're the perfect romantic couple.'

'Don't hold me so close,' she said.

'But I want to hold you close. I want to feel

your legs moving against mine, and dream of how you look beneath that dress.'

'That doesn't concern you,' she said lightly.

He tightened his hand in the small of her back, making her gasp.

'Your nakedness concerns every man in the room, and if you don't believe me, look at their faces. There isn't one of them who wouldn't take you here and now if he could.'

'But that's what you wanted—that they should envy you.'

He'd thought it was, but now he was ready to kill any man who dared turn his eyes on her. Like a malign spell, the words she'd once spoken from the depths of hatred streamed into his mind:

'...there are going to be others, make no mistake.... Are your special little touches yours alone, or do other men know them?...Never mind. I'll have fun finding out.'

'Not in a million years,' he murmured.

'What did you say?' she asked.

'Nothing. There's such a thing as propriety. Try to remember that.'

'You mean, us being such a respectable married couple. I'll do my best.'

She laughed up into his face, knowing that she

had him on the rack, and the onlookers smiled fondly to see newly-weds so adoring.

As the music slowed Vansini pounced, detaching Elise from Vincente's arms almost by force and whirling her away. The orchestra struck up again and suddenly the floor was filled with couples.

For several minutes Vansini entertained her with outrageous compliments, while also praising himself.

'I make love magnificently,' he proclaimed. 'No man is my equal, not even Vincente. Say the word and we'll put it to the test.'

'Of course,' she said. 'Any time you want my husband to bring your life to a sudden end, just let me know.'

He roared with laughter and she joined in. The onlookers murmured about how lucky Vincente was to have a wife who could get on the right side of such a useful man. They also made a pretty accurate guess at the conversation.

But then Vansini's manner changed as he noticed somebody arrive. 'My son!' he exclaimed, beaming with pride. 'At last. Come and meet him.'

He drew her across the floor to introduce her to the most astonishingly handsome young man Elise had ever seen. Carlo Vansini was tall and lithe, with a gentle charm that won her over in the first minute. She danced with him and later in the evening they fell into conversation as they ate from the buffet.

She was aware of Vincente watching her, but she pushed the thought aside. Carlo was saying things that greatly interested her. When he leaned down to speak in her ear she smiled and nodded at the thoughts he was putting into her head.

'We must meet again,' she said thoughtfully, 'and discuss this further.'

'I live for that moment,' he said gravely.

She laughed, conscious of Vincente's burning eyes on her, and returned to her other guests.

CHAPTER ELEVEN

Elise knew that she'd done well at the ball and when it was finally time to bid everyone goodnight and retire to her room she wore a smile of pleasure. There had been a development this evening that greatly pleased her. Things were looking up.

'Have you come for the diamonds?' she asked as Vincente appeared. 'It's best to lock them away as quickly as possible.'

She was removing them as she spoke, but he whisked them out of her hands and tossed them on to the bed. His face, she was delighted to notice, was that of a man at the end of his tether, and it was no surprise when he seized her in his arms.

'Shut up,' he said.

His kiss was everything she wanted—fierce, furious, desperate. She returned it, but only so far.

'Aren't you pleased with me?' she asked when she could speak. 'Did I impress your guests?'

'Too damn much,' he said against her lips.

She laughed and he released her mouth abruptly.

'I enjoyed myself,' she said. 'We have lots of dinner invitations. They all want you to take me to visit them.'

'They can want.'

'Nonsense! I'll be a prize asset. Think of how much *business* you can do.'

This was true, and the knowledge inflamed him further. How dared she talk to him of business?

'Unzip me,' she said, turning away.

He pulled the zip down, down, right down to the swell of her hips and beyond. The gorgeous black dress fell away, revealing her body to his furious eyes. She seemed unaware of his reaction, unaware of *him*, as she stepped out of the gown.

'I am really ready for a good night's sleep,' she said. 'Goodnight.'

'Goodnight?' he said, pulling her around. 'Am I expected to just go away after the performance you put on tonight?'

'That's just it. It was a performance, nothing more. To please you, I've let men fawn over me, hold me too tight, kiss my hand, but all I felt was boredom. It's amazing how boring a man can be.'

'And you're very good at the performance, aren't you?'

'As good as I have to be. I've had a lot of practice.'

'But it's not always a pretence, is it. You and I both know that.'

He was reminding her of the time he'd incited her blazing passion only to disappoint her. She hadn't been pretending then, and the knowledge lay between them now.

Vincente moved gently, laying his hand over one breast, challenging her to feel nothing. His caress was soft, almost tender, and it nearly weakened her. This was dangerous. It brought him too close to being the man she loved, and she would banish that man at all costs. He no longer belonged in her life.

'Can we have nothing for ourselves?' he whispered against her neck.

Smiling, she played her ace. 'But we do have something,' she said.

She took hold of his hand and moved it from her breast, sliding it down to lie over her stomach.

'We have this,' she said. 'Have you forgotten?'

It was true that he had forgotten. Dazzled by her, tense with frustrated desire, maddened by her elusiveness, he'd lost sight of her as a mother. Now the simple action shocked him into stillness.

The moment was gone. She was a conjurer again, waving a wand and changing herself in a flash from a siren to a matron, carrying his child. Whatever he'd been going to do, he wouldn't do it now.

'You're quite right,' he said raggedly. 'I'll leave you in peace.'

He gathered up the diamonds. Before leaving, he paused to say, 'You need not worry about my troubling you again. Goodnight.'

Elise stared at the closed door as though expecting it to open again. But it wouldn't, she knew. She'd defeated him.

'I'm winning,' she said to herself. 'I'm winning.'

But it was a hollow victory.

Vincente returned home early the next day to find that Elise was missing and nobody knew where to look for her. Mario, the chauffeur reserved for her and Mamma, knew little.

'I drove the *Signora* into town, as far as the Vatican. Then she sent me away and said she'd call when she wanted to be collected. That was four hours ago and she hasn't called.'

'She's probably just sightseeing,' Mamma tried to reassure him. 'The Vatican's a big place.'

'Of course, Mamma.'

He smiled and spoke reassuringly, but inwardly he was in turmoil. Not for one moment did he believe that Elise was sightseeing. She'd simply waited for Mario to drive away, then gone to her real destination—wherever that was and whoever she was meeting.

It meant nothing, he told himself. She was teasing him, playing one of her tricks in their private war. At any moment now she would walk in and all would be well.

But the memory intruded of her and Carlo Vansini dancing, sitting with their heads together, smiling with some private understanding.

When she returned—*if* she returned—she would shrug and refuse to admit that she'd been with him.

And he would murder her.

'Sorry, Mamma, what did you say?' he asked, pulling himself back to reality with an effort.

'I said here she is. I just saw a taxi pull up outside.'

He strode out in time to see her pay the driver. She turned and waved to him, smiling. In a searing moment he took in how beautiful she was, how perfectly presented, how suspiciously content.

'There's been a misunderstanding,' he said coldly. 'Mario said you were going to call him.'

'I was, but a taxi was passing and it was simpler to just get in.'

'Have you had a good afternoon?'

'Wonderful, thank you,' she said with a sigh of happiness.

He took her arm in a firm grip, escorted her inside and drew her into an ante-room.

'I want to know where you've been,' he said through gritted teeth.

'Boy, you really come out of the nineteenth century, don't you! Yes, my lord and master. No, my lord and master.'

'I said I want to know where you've been— and who with.'

She gave him a look that, if he hadn't been so wrought up, he might have recognised as pity.

'I've spent the afternoon in my apartment,' she said.

'Alone?'

'No, with Carlo Vansini.'

His face grew hard. 'You dare to stand there and admit it in that brazen way?' he snapped.

'What's brazen about it?' she asked innocently. 'Selling property is a perfectly respectable occupation.'

'Selling—?'

'Oh, Vincente, if you could only see your face! I've sold Carlo my apartment. It was exactly what he was looking for. He told me last night he wanted a place where he could have a private life. He finds living with his mother a bit inhibiting.'

Vincente couldn't speak. Something had caught in his throat.

'I told him I had a place for sale,' she went on, 'and we agreed to meet there this afternoon. He loved it at once.'

'That's where you've been?' he asked.

'Of course. What's the matter?'

'You never thought to tell me first?'

'Why should I? I don't need your permission.'

But that wasn't why and they both knew it. She'd put him through hell for the fun of it, or perhaps to make a point.

'Besides, I didn't want to risk you putting off another buyer,' she added.

'Why should I do that? I know I did last time, but things are different now.'

'Not really. You're still trying to control me. The money I'll get is my independence, and I'm going to have that, make no mistake. Carlo and I went to the agent and told him to put the sale through fast. He's anxious to take possession at once, so the money should be through in a week. Then I'll be able to pay off all my debts, including my debts to you.'

'You owe me nothing.'

'That's not true. After that, I went to the lawyer, and he let slip about all the bills Ben left outstanding, that you've been paying. That's very kind of

you—' but she didn't sound as if she really considered it kind '—but you'll get every last penny
back, with interest. I'll still have enough left to
start my own business when I've finished my
fashion course.'

'Business? When I can buy you everything you
want?'

She met his eyes and said softly, 'The thing I
want most is something you can't buy me,
Vincente. Don't you know that by now?'

That silenced him.

She moved away, saying, 'I want my independence, my freedom. I'll still be here. You'll have
your wife and your child, but I'll be free.'

He didn't answer. He seemed to be considering.

To soften the atmosphere, she said, 'How could
you think—what you were thinking?'

'Because I don't know you,' he said simply. 'I
don't know who you are any more.'

'You never did. At least now you recognise it.
By the way, the estate agent asked me to give
you a message. He thinks he has a buyer for
your own flat.'

'Good.'

'So now we're even. You didn't tell me that you
were selling, either.'

'Tell you? And have you crow over me?' He

managed to say this with a very faint glimmer of humour. Inwardly, relief was sending him slightly crazy.

'I wouldn't do that. When did you put it on the market?'

'The day you agreed to marry me.'

'There was no need for you to sell, if it was because of a foolish joke I once made—'

'About the legions of women I could entertain there? I haven't the slightest wish to do that.' In a voice heavy with irony he added, 'I'm a devoted family man now.'

'Ah, yes! Ruthless entrepreneur, man about town, the complete many-sided image. But it's a good idea to adjust one of the sides now and then. I congratulate you.'

His face darkened. 'You know better than that.'

'Do I?'

'Unless you're very stupid, and I never thought you were. Not before this. All I want now is you and our child.'

'And you've acquired us very thoroughly. Well done.'

It was like trying to argue with steel, he thought grimly. But who could he blame but himself?

Both sales went through quickly. At her insistence Vincente accepted the money she owed him, but there was still enough left to make her feel that she could have a life of her own.

Life at the Palazzo was more pleasant than she had feared, chiefly because her mother-in-law adored her. When she had a giddy spell it was Elise she clung to until the doctor appeared and ordered her to bed. And it was Elise who promised faithfully not to disturb Vincente, and then promptly broke a promise she'd never intended to keep by calling him at the office.

Luckily he was there, and able to return home at once. Mamma chided Elise for her disobedience, but her eyes shone with affection.

Later that night Vincente knocked on her door. 'May I come in for a few minutes?'

She'd already undressed for bed and was wearing a silk nightdress and robe, but he showed no awareness of this as she stood back to let him pass, and even seemed to avoid looking at her.

'I just wanted to thank you for taking care of Mamma,' he said.

'No need. I thought being here would be difficult but she's easy to love.'

'Yes, she makes a lot of things tolerable,' he agreed, changing her meaning slightly, knowing she would understand.

'Elise,' he said suddenly, 'have you looked ahead, down the years, to the kind of marriage we're going to have?'

'You'll be a good father, I know that. You do everything efficiently once you've set your mind to it.'

He looked at her, wearing the soft silk that seemed to conceal her body while actually suggesting so much, and he remembered the times when she would have thrown it aside and opened her arms to him.

He wondered if she realised that she was standing against the light from the bedside lamp, so that the material became transparent, revealing her perfect shape beneath. It was still early in her pregnancy and, beyond a slight extra voluptuousness, her shape was unchanged.

Efficiently. Did she know how the word savaged him?

He knew he ought to leave now while he was still in some sort of control of himself. The other night she'd dared him to take her in anger, and they'd both known he couldn't do that. Not now. But if she would soften to him there was still hope.

He moved towards her, close enough to lay a gentle hand on her cheek. It was a touch she'd always loved, just as he had always loved the slight *frisson* he could sense inside her when he did it.

Now there was nothing. She might have been made of stone. He escaped quickly.

A few days later a large box was delivered to the house. Later that night Elise told Vincente quietly, 'I'd like to talk to you before you go to bed.'

When he called in her room she handed him an envelope.

'When I came to Rome I left a lot of things in store in England. I sent for them recently and they arrived today. This is the letter I wrote Angelo, the one Ben stole. I want you to read it.'

'Are you sure?'

'Quite sure.'

He took it slowly and turned away to the window. He wanted to read it, yet he desperately wanted to refuse.

It was as terrible as he'd feared. For the first time he saw Elise as she had been then, pouring out her heart with all the fervour and passion of young love and grief at parting.

Try to forgive me, my darling…I never meant it to be this way…

She told the whole story, just as she had told it to Vincente: how Ben had arrived suddenly in Rome and snatched her away, using threats to her father.

I heard you calling under my window and I tried to call back to you, to let you know that you were the one I loved…but he gripped me so tightly I couldn't escape…I love you, I shall always love you…try to forgive me…forgive… forgive…

'If you showed me this to prove that I misjudged you,' he said, 'there was no need. I've known that a long time. I didn't want to know it. When you first came to Rome—and we were together—I tried not to see what was happening to me, but in the end I had to face it. I wanted you to be innocent, so that I could love you without feeling guilty.'

'That's the trouble.' She sighed. 'Guilt destroys everything. I live with my guilt all the time, and there's hardly anything of me left. I don't feel anything any more.'

'Don't say that.'

'It's true. I prefer it that way. It's safer. Perhaps we might have loved each other if we'd met differently—'

'There's no perhaps about it,' he said harshly. 'We were meant to love each other, despite all the things that came between us. Sooner or later, you have to accept that.'

'Have to?' She shook her head firmly. 'No, I don't

"have to". Don't try to give me orders, Vincente. This is one thing that isn't in your control. I won't love you. I can't, and if I could, I wouldn't.'

'And suppose I love you,' he snapped furiously.

How different this might have been. Once her face would have softened with joy at a hint of love. Now she merely gave a sad little sigh and said, 'Then you're unfortunate. What right have I to be happy with you or any man, when Angelo lies in his grave and I put him there?'

'But you were innocent,' he said passionately.

'How can I be? But for me he'd be alive. That's the plain truth of it and all the rest is talk. You were right to hate me.'

'I never hated you,' he said in a low voice.

She smiled then. She actually smiled.

'You must have forgotten a great deal. You hunted me down, hating me. You lured me into a trap, hating me. You watched me struggle, hating me. You took me to bed, hating me. You did something that you made me think was love-making, but actually you were studying me all the time, always in control, watching to see if the moment had come to destroy me.'

'*No!*' he said violently. 'That's how it was meant to be, not how it was. You were different from everything I'd expected—I tried not to see it, but it was too much for me. *You* were too much for me. If you hadn't found out when you did, I was going to tell you everything.'

'That's a delusion. There's no way you could ever have told me.'

'It would have been hard. That's why I was putting it off, but I'd have found a way because I knew we had to be together.'

'Well, we are together,' she said, sighing.

Together? They stood staring at each other, while the distance between them stretched wide.

He looked again at the letter.

'"Try to forgive me,"' he read aloud. '"Forgive… forgive…"'

He came closer. 'Can you never forgive? We both said things that were cruel and harsh, but surely you know now that I meant none of them?'

'They were true anyway.' She sighed.

'Angelo loved you. He wouldn't want you to suffer like this for something you couldn't help.'

'Don't,' she whispered, covering her eyes. 'Don't talk to me about him, I can't bear it. I thought I'd learned to live with the worst, but I didn't know what the worst was. I never knew I'd killed him, but I should have guessed it was something like that.'

'You didn't kill him,' Vincente raged.

'As good as. I drove him to it. I killed him. In

here—' she pounded her chest with a clenched fist '—I know I killed him, and nothing's ever going to change that.'

A violent sob broke from her, making him go to her. At that moment he would have done anything to ease her pain. But he was the last man who could help her. He touched her but she immediately dried her tears.

'You know—' she sighed '—if I seem to hate you, it's mostly because I hate myself.'

'What are we going to do?' he said quietly.

'I don't know,' she said sadly. 'I'm not sure that there's anything to be done.'

Summer moved on through the heat of August and September. Elise's health was good and, despite her increasing size, she coped with the high temperatures well.

Not that everything was easy. There was one terrible evening when Mamma insisted on the three of them celebrating Angelo's birthday. He would have been twenty-nine.

The evening was an endurance test. Mamma had looked at every photograph she possessed of him. Elise went through them nervously, dreading to find one that chanced to show herself.

In this, at least, she was lucky. There was

nothing to give away her secret. She gazed at the face of her young love, looking back at her with an endless smile.

Then she looked up at Vincente, and found him regarding her with desperation.

That night he slipped into her room without knocking, as he usually did.

'I'm sorry,' he said at once. 'I had no idea that was going to happen.'

'I suppose it's because I was here. She said she wanted to "introduce me" to Angelo. Never mind, it's over now, and it gave her a little happiness.'

He said abruptly, 'You're rather wonderful, d'you know that?'

She turned away so that he wouldn't see how affected she was by something in his voice that she'd never heard before. Passion, laughter, these she was used to, but the note of gentle admiration she heard now caught her off guard.

'I'd like to go to sleep now,' she said. 'Goodnight.'

'Goodnight.' He hesitated. 'Thank you for everything.'

He kissed her cheek and was gone.

Elise lay down, trying to clear her mind of the smiling images of Angelo that she'd seen that day.

But he pursued her even in sleep, and she awoke to find herself crying aloud.

'Hush,' said Vincente's voice close by in the darkness. 'It's all right.'

She found that she was sobbing and could barely speak. 'What happened?'

'You were calling out in your sleep. I heard you and I thought I'd better come in. You might have called his name aloud.'

So he'd known who was in her dreams, she thought.

'Does he trouble you very much?' Vincente asked quietly.

'I feel guilty about him all the time.'

He said nothing. Her answer didn't tell him what he really wanted to know. Did she dream of Angelo with longing? Was he, after all that had happened, still her one true love?

He waited for her to say more, but after a while he felt her head grow heavy against his shoulder and her breathing become slower. She had fallen asleep again.

He kissed the top of her head.

'It's all right,' he said again, tightening his arms. 'I'm here.'

After a while he laid her gently down and pulled the sheet up over her. Taking care not to awaken her, he left the room noiselessly, returned to his own room and took out his cellphone.

'Razzini?' he said softly. 'Yes, I know it's late. Wake up, man.'

Razzini's voice rasped down the line. 'Signore Farnese? I never expected to hear from you again. The last time we met you were ready to kill me.'

'I still might, but first I have a job for you. And it's urgent, so drop everything else.'

'That won't be easy—'

'Yes, it will, for the price I'll pay. I want your undivided attention. You'll work on this, day and night, until you can tell me what I want to know.'

'Sounds important.'

'It is important,' Vincente said sombrely. 'It's a matter of life and death.'

Paradoxically, as she grew larger Elise also felt stronger. As Christmas neared and Vincente embarked on a spate of business entertaining, she flowered, taking a full part in the preparations.

After one particularly lively evening he called at her room to say goodnight.

'My friends admire you very much,' he said. 'You couldn't have done better. Are you all right?'

'Yes, just a little tired.' She patted her

stomach. 'I shall be glad when this is over. He's very lively.'

'Or she.'

'No, definitely a he. From the way he's kicking, this is a footballer.'

'Perhaps I should stay in case something happens.'

'Nothing will happen for another two months. I'm fine.'

'Babies have been known to come early,' he persisted.

She laughed. 'If those men out there could see you now! They're all afraid of you.'

'And I'd like them to go on being afraid of me.'

'Then I won't tell them what a fusspot you can be.'

'They wouldn't believe you,' he said simply. 'Nobody but you has ever seen me like this. Nobody else ever will.'

'Silence, I swear it. Look, here's the buzzer you gave me. If anything happens I'll press it and wake you.'

'Be sure you do.'

As she bid him goodnight her smile held a touch of fondness. These days a blessed peace had crept over her, so that it was possible to relax and detach herself from sadness, even to feel content with him. She knew he sometimes slipped into her room at night to hold her when the bad dreams came, but he didn't stay long, and they never spoke of it by day.

It was February when the birth began. Vincente took her to the hospital and stood back, waiting as they settled Elise in the side ward. She turned her head, needing to keep him in sight all the time. A pain went through her.

'The contractions are coming fast,' somebody said. 'This won't take long.'

The pain was sharp, which had the strange effect of sharpening her mind. Through a brilliant light she seemed to see him standing there, just like before, when she'd first come to this hospital and nearly lost their child. She'd known then that he wouldn't come to her unless she asked, and nothing would have made her ask.

But it was different now. Her hand went out to him, seeking, inviting, imploring. He was there at once, his grip giving her the message she longed for.

'Don't leave me,' she begged.

'Never,' he whispered.

In the same moment the pain came again, making her tighten her fingers on his so that he actually winced.

'Sorry,' she gasped.

'It's fine if it makes you feel better. Can't I take some of it away from you?'

She was about to tell him that pain didn't work like that but, mysteriously, it did, for there was comfort to be found in his supporting clasp, and even more in his eyes, watching her with fond anxiety.

The contractions came again and again, growing more frequent as the moment neared. Even so, Vincente demanded frantically of the doctor, 'Can't you hurry it up?' which made everyone laugh, including Elise.

'I think you should leave this to me,' she suggested.

'No, we're in it together,' he said seriously.

'Then get ready,' she screamed suddenly. And the next moment the baby was there.

'It's a girl,' said the doctor.

'Is she all right?' Elise asked urgently.

His reply was drowned out by a furious yell from the mite in his hands.

'Fit and healthy,' he said, raising his voice in order to be heard.

They cleaned the baby and wrapped her in a shawl, but it was Vincente who took her and carried her to the bed, to lay her in her mother's arms. Elise held her in silence, awed that this tiny scrap had drawn its life from the two of them, months ago when they had known the beginning of love, before it had been beaten down, almost to nothing.

Almost.

A nurse wheeled in a cot and settled her in it. Vincente went to look down at the baby.

'Would you have preferred a son?' she asked.

He shook his head, not taking his eyes from the child. 'No, this is better,' he said. A sudden smile breaking over his face, he looked down at his daughter. 'She smiled at me.'

'That's impossible; she's only a few minutes old. They don't smile for weeks.'

'My daughter isn't like other children,' he said firmly. 'She can do anything.'

Elise watched him tenderly, loving him for what she could tell was happening. Already she could see how this birth could help to heal old wounds.

Yet the ghost was still there. She'd sensed it when Vincente had said, 'This is better.' He'd meant it was better not to have a son since Mamma had set her heart on calling him Angelo. And Elise had understood him at once.

While that was true there would never be the true peace between them that both of them wanted.

She gave a soft sigh as weariness closed in. It wouldn't have surprised her if, absorbed in the miracle in the cot, Vincente had failed to hear her.

But he was beside her at once, laying his lips gently on her forehead.

'Thank you,' he murmured as she slid into sleep. 'Thank you for everything—my love.'

CHAPTER TWELVE

ELISE stepped under the shower and stood, relishing the water that splashed over her, enjoying the thought of what was to come.

In a few days' time her three-month-old daughter would be christened in the same church where she herself had been married, but this was going to be a big occasion, with the church packed to the rafters.

It was Mamma who had insisted on calling the baby Olivia, which was Elise's second name. The child had fulfilled everybody's hopes, bringing new life to Mamma and a new softening to Vincente. He adored his daughter and spent every possible moment in her company, with the result that his best hopes had been realised and her first smile had been his.

The atmosphere between them now was amiable, but still wary. They knew they were standing at a crossroads, but the lanes stretched out of sight. Both were waiting for something to happen. As time passed her figure had regained its shape, her strength had returned and she had become more and more aware of how long it had been since they had made love.

She could use the term love-making to herself now. The love had always been there, and perhaps was still there, but it wouldn't easily be tempted out of hiding.

Often she caught him watching her silently, as though reminding her of the closeness they had shared at the birth, and asking where it would lead. At any moment, she was sure, he would let her know that he wanted her in his bed. But nothing happened. If he met her eyes he'd turn his own away. The door to her room was unlocked, but these days he never tried it.

She shivered at the thought that perhaps he was content with this situation, that he no longer wanted her.

There was a long mirror beside the bath and, as she stepped out, it showed her whole length. She paused and looked herself over, recalling another occasion when she'd studied herself. On the day of her arrival in Rome she'd showered and considered her own nakedness because she had wanted to see herself through Vincente's eyes.

She'd wanted him so badly. The weeks of lonely denial in England hadn't altered the fact that her thoughts had been in Italy, with him, and all that mattered had been to make him desire her.

Then her figure had been elegant, almost boyish. Now the birth had left her more rounded, almost voluptuous, in a way that she instinctively knew that Vincente would like.

'The perfect woman,' he'd told her once, long ago, 'is always changing, so there's always something new to relish.' His eyes had glimmered as he'd teased her. 'And then he can have a new experience without the boring inconvenience of being unfaithful.'

She'd laughed and slapped him lightly. The next moment she'd been flat on her back on the bed while he lay on top of her.

'Rough stuff, eh?' he'd observed. 'Two can play at that game.'

He'd then treated her to the most vigorous sex they had ever enjoyed, but when it was over it was he who had the scratch marks and she who had been apologetic.

Remembering it now, Elise smiled, then suppressed the smile as soon as she saw it reflected. Happy memories only led to more melancholy.

He'd joked about infidelity, but had he been faithful to her recently? She cast her mind back, trying to recall any unexplained absences, but there were none. He was always home early. It meant nothing, she told herself, almost determined not to think well of him. He could have done anything during the day, and she would never know.

But somehow that picture did not convince her. He was waiting, just as she was.

She was about to reach for the big towel when the bathroom door opened behind her. She whirled and saw him there, thunderstruck as he took in the full glory of her nakedness. For a moment they looked at each other without moving.

'I'm sorry,' he said in a harsh voice. 'I didn't know you were in here.'

Vincente backed out quickly and slammed the door.

It was all over in seconds but the effect was shattering. There in his face was everything she'd wanted to see—longing, loneliness, above all a desire so fierce that he'd been on the verge of taking her there and then.

But he'd conquered it, because by proving himself stronger than temptation he sent her a message of finality. She might be the most beautiful, sexually devastating woman in the world, but he would resist her because that was what he had decided to do. And his decisions were final.

Elise had no choice but to accept that, and confront him with the same. Their trial of strength had moved into a new phase, but it hadn't come to an end.

Now she resented him for the way her body was thrumming with the thoughts and feelings he'd put there but refused to satisfy. For four years she'd lived untouched by Ben or any other man, had cared nothing, but this was a new woman, the one Vincente had brought to life, and her flesh screamed for his intimate caresses.

After a while she wrapped the towel around herself and returned to her room, moving quietly, not to alert him.

Vincente opened wide the windows of his bedroom, drawing back the curtains so that he could look out at the huge grounds, and let the faint breeze touch him. It wasn't enough to cool him down. Nothing could do that.

With the lamp turned out there was only a faint hint of moonlight, casting a glimmer on a small part of the room and throwing the rest into black shadows. Throwing aside his clothes, he dropped on to the huge bed and lay on his back, staring up at the dark ceiling.

The click of the door was so soft that at first he wasn't sure he'd heard it. But then there came another click as the door closed, and he turned his head slowly on the pillow.

A naked woman stood in the darkness. He could only just make out her shape, but he would have known her anywhere and lay, transfixed, as Elise approached noiselessly until she could stand looking down at him.

She paused for a long time while he wondered what was holding her back. She could have no doubts about her welcome. His arousal was fierce and hard, and just visible in the faintest moonlight, but she seemed to want to make sure because she reached out a gentle finger, caressing its whole length lightly and giving a faint sigh that might have been satisfaction.

'Don't start this if you don't mean it,' he said hoarsely.

She made no sound, but dropped on to the bed beside him, letting her hand drift here and there, following its own sweet will. He tried to reach up and pull her closer, but she prevented him, and he just made out a shake of her head.

Then he felt her finger placed lightly over his mouth and he understood. Whatever happened tonight was for her to say. If he disobeyed, she might vanish for ever, leaving behind only the respectable wife and mother that he'd made of her, when he wanted more—much, much more. He wanted the mischievous genie that lurked inside her, and he wanted to possess it completely—or at least until it vanished, to make him wait for the next time.

That was his last coherent thought. From then on thoughts and sensations swam into each other. Her hand continued to tease him, but absent-mindedly, as though she had other matters to think of. She pulled back again until she was in an upright position. He could see her hair hanging down, but her face was in darkness, except for an occasional gleam from her eyes.

'Don't make me wait,' he groaned.

For answer she swung a leg over him and settled down so that he was enclosed inside her, not by his will but by hers. He waited for her to lean down against him, but she sat there, high up, proud and haughty, regarding his subjection with lofty enjoyment.

Now he could just make out her mouth, and the wicked smile that curved it—a smile that said, You're mine and I'm going to make sure you know it.

Her hips were working powerfully, rising and falling, showing no mercy. A long groan broke from him. He arched his back, throwing his head backwards, and then she was stretched out on him, claiming his mouth with her own, still in control but finally offering the rest of her body to his embrace—the generosity of the victor.

Let her be the winner, then. Let her have anything she wanted as long as she could bring his heart and body alive as no other woman had ever done.

She seemed possessed of inhuman stamina, taking them both to the heights twice, three times. When she slid softly on to the bed beside him he tried to embrace her, but she was suddenly insubstantial and slipped from his grasp.

He felt only the lightest touch of her lips. Then she vanished into the darkness.

He lay peacefully, bathed in the joy of what had happened, trying to believe it. A new path had opened up for them, one that might lead to peace and happiness.

But there was still something missing, a grief in her heart that must be put to rest before her happiness could be complete. With all his soul he longed to make her that gift in return for what she had given him, but who knew if or when it would happen?

The phone beside the bed rang and he answered it.

'It's me,' said Razzini's voice. 'I've got what you wanted.'

* * *

Vincente and Elise met at breakfast the next morning but, in Mamma's presence, neither of them gave any hint of what had happened the night before.

Watching Elise's slightly alarming self posses-sion, Vincente wondered if he might actually be delusional, but the relaxed feeling that had infused his body when he'd awoken told its own story.

Then he pulled himself together. What he had to do today was vital, and might transform their whole lives. He left before breakfast was over.

He didn't return that evening and there was still no sign of him when Elise went to bed. Lying awake in the early hours, she heard him creep into his room, making only the careful noises of a man who didn't want to awaken anyone.

Fine, she thought angrily. If that was how he wanted to play it—*fine*! She turned over and fell into a furious sleep.

But the next morning he said to her, 'I want to take you somewhere.'

'Where?'

Vincente hesitated. 'Trust me.'

When they were in the car she said, 'Isn't this the way to the church?'

'Yes. There's someone I want you to meet.'

When they arrived he led her into the church-yard, but not into the building. Instead, he turned aside and headed for Angelo's grave. To her surprise, Elise saw two men there—one weedy and middle-aged, the other youngish and dishevelled. He was sitting down, leaning back against the headstone, his face unshaven, his hair untidy, his clothes slovenly. As they approached he took a long drag on something that he was smoking. He seemed oblivious to the outside world.

'What's he doing there?' Elise demanded indignantly. 'Who is he, and who's that horrid little man?'

'The horrid little man is Razzini, and he's the best private investigator in the business.'

'Private investigator?' She stopped. 'Is he the one you hired to find me?'

'Yes, I told you he's the best. *No!*' He gripped her as she tried to turn away. 'You mustn't go.'

'If you think I want—what are you playing at? How dare you do this?'

'Elise, please—*please* don't leave. This is important. It matters more than anything ever has before. You must talk to him.'

'Tell me why.'

'I can't. You have to hear it from that young man. Elise, I *beg* you to trust me.'

She would have protested, but something in his eyes refused to be denied. This was the crossroads she had sensed approaching, and there were so many directions to take. But he was still holding her, drawing her along his chosen path, which might or might not be the right one.

'I swear I would die before hurting you again,' he said urgently. *'Trust me!'*

'All right,' she whispered. 'I will trust you. I do.'

Not releasing her, he drew her along the path, talking gently. 'I'd hoped for this to happen earlier, but it's taken Razzini months to track that lad down.'

'And you told him to?'

'I had to. I wanted to know how Angelo died. Because we don't know. Not really. We know he drove off and was found dead, and we've all made our assumptions, but there didn't seem to be any witnesses. I told Razzini to move heaven and earth to find someone who could tell us more. That young man is Franco Danzi, and he knows everything.'

As he drew her closer, Razzini turned to them. 'At last.'

They all looked at the young man, sprawled against the stone.

'Get up,' Vincente said, hauling him to his feet. 'There's no need to insult the dead.'

'I do the best I can,' was the strange reply. 'I'd much rather insult Angelo alive. He ruined my life, and I can't even pay him back as he deserves.'

He gave Vincente a bleary gaze. 'We've met before, haven't we? You came to see me in prison.'

'Yesterday. We had a long talk.'

'Ah, yes, I remember now. You're Angelo's cousin and I'm—'

'Your name is Franco Danzi,' Vincente reminded him with a touch of pity.

'That's right. Not that it matters. I barely have a name these days. Why should you remember it? Why should anyone? The prison authorities know it. They let me out this morning and said don't come back. But I expect I will. I've nowhere else to go, and it's his fault.'

He jabbed at the headstone.

'I thought we were friends,' Franco said in a whining voice. 'But he was the one who got me started on these.' He waved the thing he was smoking which, from its smell, was far more than an ordinary cigarette.

'That's not true,' Elise said fiercely. 'Angelo never touched drugs.'

'That's right, he didn't,' Franco agreed. 'He was worse than that. He stayed clean himself, but he lured other people in so that he could make money. His family had money, but he said he wanted to get his own and be his own master.'

'You're lying,' Elise said bitterly.

When Vincente said nothing she looked at him with indignation.

'You don't mean you believe all this?' she demanded.

'I didn't when he first told me. Like you, I couldn't square it with my picture of Angelo. But I've been thinking, and now I do believe. It explains some things that puzzled me at the time. Suddenly he'd be flush with money that he couldn't account for, except to say that he'd won it gambling. But it happened too often.

'Briefly he worked for me in the firm, but he was idle and self-indulgent, and he left just before I was going to fire him. I think it left him bitter.'

'Bitter? He was furious,' Franco said. 'Then he started dealing, and he said it was the first thing he'd been a real success at. Oh, he was a success all right. He got his friends hooked. He thought it was all going to be easy, but Gianni didn't like it.'

'Gianni?' Elise queried.

'That's how everyone knew him. He didn't need a surname. You just had to say "Gianni" and people trembled. He was the big dealer in this area, and he warned Angelo off his patch, but Angelo wouldn't take any notice. So Gianni killed him.'

Elise tensed. 'But surely—he killed himself?'

Franco gave a mirthless laugh. 'Don't tell me

you've been fooled by that story too. How he saw his girlfriend in the arms of another man, and was so heartbroken that he ended it all? Oh, he saw her all right. I know. I was there. And I'm not saying he wasn't upset, because he was. But he wasn't suicidal. He just wanted to get drunk.

'He stormed off to his car, cursing his head off, and I had to run to keep up with him. I only just managed it and got in as he started up. I saw the other car pull out and follow us. Even in the dark I knew it was Gianni. He had this fancy car that you could spot anywhere. He came chasing after us. Angelo went faster and faster, trying to outrun him, but he couldn't.

'I could see how it was going to end, so I jumped out. Luckily we were out in the country by then and I landed on grass. I rolled down a bank, got knocked out and didn't wake up for hours. Next thing I heard, Angelo was dead. They found his car smashed up and it took hours to free him. He didn't do it himself. Gianni drove him off the road as a warning to others. He'd done it before to people who got in his way. We all knew.'

'And you never told anyone?' Elise asked, pale.

'And have Gianni come after me? Are you crazy? I've never been so scared in my life. I went into hiding and for weeks I just took every drug I could lay my hands on. I don't know how long I was out of it, but when I finally came round I knew my last hope of getting clean was gone.'

'So Gianni got away with murder?' Elise demanded angrily.

'Not for long. He died three years later when someone did much the same to him that he'd done to Angelo. Only a lot nastier.'

'Good,' she said quietly, and Vincente gave her a look of admiration.

He handed a thick envelope to Razzini. 'You've done a good job. Take this, and call me if you ever need anything.'

Razzini stared. 'What did you say?'

'I said you can come to me for help. I owe you.'

Razzini took the envelope, checked the contents and gave a satisfied grunt.

'What about him?' he asked, indicating Franco.

'You can leave him with me.'

Franco had simply given up, sliding to the ground, muttering.

'Go on, call the police. I could just use a nice comfortable cell.'

'How about a nice comfortable bed in a rehab centre?' Vincente suggested.

'As if they'd have me!'

'I think they will,' Vincente said, looking up to

where the priest was walking towards them. 'Father, if you can find a place for him in one of the church's centres I'll pay all his expenses.'

'You already make generous donations—'

'This will be in addition. I think my family owes him something. Please get him away from here and into a safe place.'

Two young priests came hurrying out to help haul the now comatose Franco away. Elise stood watching them, unable to move. What she had just discovered had left her numb. From some distant place she had a sensation that everything was different. A burden had been lifted from her and, although it was too soon to feel relief, she knew that relief would come.

Not merely relief. Freedom. She'd hurt Angelo, but she hadn't killed him. A miracle had saved her from a lifetime of suffering, and it was Vincente who had made it happen.

'Elise.' Vincente gently took her shoulders.

She opened her eyes.

'Free,' she whispered. 'It's true, isn't it?'

'I think it must be. As I said, it explains things I didn't understand at the time.'

'Then it wasn't my fault,' she whispered.

'No, it wasn't. None of it was your fault. Let's go home.'

She sat quietly in the car, trying to understand what was happening, that a brighter future was opening up for them, but what she felt most intensely was a feeling of joy that started deep inside her and grew until it filled the world.

But it was too soon to give herself up to it. As Mamma came to meet them they shared a glance, silently agreeing that she must be protected from this revelation. The truth cleared Elise, but would only increase Mamma's grief. They both hugged her and spoke warmly of tomorrow's celebrations.

When they all retired for the night Elise stopped at her bedroom door and held out her hand. He followed her in, but he didn't immediately take her in his arms.

'Did it really happen?' she murmured.

'Yes, it happened,' he said, sitting beside her. 'And it gives us a chance we might never have had. Now we can emerge from the shadows and find each other.'

'I was crushed by the weight of my own guilt. I thought I'd killed him. I didn't believe that you could ever truly forgive me.'

Vincente shook his head. 'It's you that needs to forgive. When I look back on myself, the things I did, the deception I practised on you—

I'm filled with shame. My rage and bitterness were so great that I thought of nothing else. I told myself that whatever I did was right because my cause was just.

'And so I shut down all decent feelings for years. By the time I found you I was so obsessed that I could think of nothing else but my revenge, and my own rightness. But you—you changed everything. That very first evening, I knew things weren't as I'd thought for so long, but I wouldn't let myself believe it.

'I clung to my illusions even while you cast your spell over me. I had to find a way to draw you into my life because I needed you to save me.'

'Save you?'

'I know now that by that time I was almost beyond hope, dead to most normal human feeling. But you awakened me, brought me back to life, taught me how to love again, as only you could have done.

'When I knew I was falling in love with you I fought it with all my strength. Thank God I failed. It was too strong for me, and when I gave in to it I knew such a blessed sense of ease and freedom. It was right as nothing else had ever been.

'I knew I must soon tell you everything, but I always drew back because you would condemn me, justly. Then I might lose you for ever, and that would be the worst thing that could happen. I kept saying, just a little longer, trying to make you fall as deeply in love with me as I was with you.'

'Love?' she whispered.

A tender smile overtook his face as he softly brushed her cheek. 'Didn't you know long ago that I loved you? Wasn't it obvious?'

'There was a time when you took trouble not to let me know.'

'Of course. I thought it would give you the whip hand over me, and I couldn't risk that. I still had so much to learn in those days.'

'Me too,' she said wryly. 'I wanted the upper hand as well—just in case.'

'But where the love is real, there's no "just in case",' he said urgently, 'no putting up defences against the dangers of commitment. But the dangers have to be faced if the love is to last. I know that now, but in those days I was still finding my way to you, step by step.

'When I was away I came back to you like a creature seeking its home. My body needed you, and I could know no peace until we'd lain together again, but my heart needed you a hundred times more. The more I loved you, the more worried I became, because I could see how easy it would be to lose you.

'And I mustn't lose you, my beloved, because that might send me back to the man I was becoming. And I don't ever want to be like him again.'

'So who are you now?' she asked tenderly.

'I'm the man you want me to be, whoever and whatever he is. I'm not even sure myself, but you can show me.'

'That's a terrible power you're putting into my hands,' she said. 'It's scary.'

'I'm not afraid, as long as it's your hands and nobody else's.'

'If I hadn't learned the truth as I did,' she mused, 'I wonder what would have happened.'

'Don't remind me of that night,' he said with soft vehemence. 'I never meant to say those terrible things to you. I was reacting to your anger. I'd have said anything to hurt you, but I regretted it bitterly afterwards. I knew that I loved you, but I was trapped in my own web. Once I'd started, I didn't know how to stop.'

'I seem to recall that I gave as good as I got,' she mused.

'I think you were possessed by the devil. When you taunted me with the men you were planning to have in the future I nearly went insane. Since then I've been jealous to the point of madness.

Even when you were heavy with child it made no difference. I saw men look at you, I read their minds and I wanted to kill.

'And you enjoyed tormenting me. That day you sold the apartment and let me think—' He broke off, shaking his head in confusion at the memory.

'Of course I enjoyed tormenting you,' she said, smiling. 'And I always will. Don't think the years ahead are going to be easy for you.'

'Let them be anything you say. Only tell me that you can love me, that you can forgive me for everything I've done.'

'I forgave you long ago,' she assured him. 'I was wrong to blame you as much as I did. It was as though we were both caught up in a whirlwind, neither of us in control.'

'I know. I was in despair, thinking there was no way out.'

'But you discovered one,' she said in wonder. 'If you hadn't looked for Franco this would have hung over us all our lives.'

'It was the only thing I could do for you to atone for what I did in the beginning. You weren't the only one carrying a load of guilt, but in my case it was deserved. I knew that while you were wretched I could never be happy. I can't think of myself as separate from you. We have to be one person, or we're nothing. My life is yours, Elise. Do with it as you will.'

She didn't answer in words, but she put her arms about him, not passionately but resting her head against his shoulder, knowing she had finally taken the right road and come home. He held her in silence, sensing her thoughts, sharing them.

'Do you mind very much about Angelo?' he asked at last, fearful of the answer.

She drew away so that she could look him in the face, shaking her head.

'But for Angelo we wouldn't have met,' she said. 'And that would have been a tragedy, because you are the only man I shall ever want in my heart. If I hadn't discovered what I did today, I should still have loved you, but in pain. But today frees me from the burden.'

Now she could say the words that had waited so long. 'I love you, Vincente, and I shall always love you.'

'Always,' he echoed. 'Promise me that.'

'Always.'

'Stay with me and love me for ever. I won't let you go. I'll fight to my last breath to keep you mine, and woe betide anyone who challenges me.'

She laughed fondly. 'What became of the new man? That sounds just like the old Vincente.'

'I never said I was going to be different to the rest of the world. Only in here—' he laid his hand over his heart '—just for you, and Olivia.'

Suddenly he gave a brilliant smile, full of joy. 'We haven't said goodnight to her yet.'

The nursery was next door to her room. As they went in the nursemaid rose and slipped through the door to her own room, leaving them alone with the baby.

'She's fast asleep,' Vincente murmured, sitting beside the cot and looking down on his daughter with the tender smile that Elise loved. To her and to his child he would offer that vulnerable face. But not to anybody else.

He leaned down to bestow a gentle kiss on the little forehead. Olivia gurgled but didn't awaken.

'Goodnight,' Elise whispered, kissing her.

'She's so peaceful,' Vincente said as they returned to Elise's room. 'I envy her that peace. I once thought that you and I would never know it. Can we find it now? Can we put the past behind us and forget what happened?'

But she was wiser and she shook her head. 'I don't want to forget everything,' she said. 'There's too much that was beautiful, and in the bad times we learned to understand each other. We'll need that in the years to come, because they aren't going to be dull years.'

'Not with us,' he agreed wryly. 'But we don't have to fight, do we?'

'I think perhaps we do,' she said, considering. 'Fighting can be—very interesting.' She gave the last words a special meaning.

'Yes,' he said, understanding, 'I've missed our battles—and the aftermath.'

She gave him a wicked smile. 'You haven't entirely gone without, have you?' she teased. 'I heard a rumour about some shameless hussy who flitted through here recently—but perhaps that didn't really happen.'

'I'm not quite sure whether it happened or not,' he mused, catching her tone. 'She didn't leave a name.'

'So you wouldn't know her again?'

'I'd know her anywhere,' he murmured. 'She was unforgettable.'

'Should I be jealous?'

'Not for a moment.'

'Did she look anything like me?'

He considered, but shook his head. 'No, she wasn't wearing as much as you.'

Her fingers were already working on her dress. A moment later it was tossed aside.

'More like that?'

'Better,' he agreed.

He removed the rest for her. There was a light in his eyes that she hadn't seen for a long while, and it made her heart beat faster.

'Tell me what happened,' she whispered.

'I was lying on my bed...'

'Fully dressed?'

'I don't...think so.'

Her hands were busy. 'Tell me when to stop.'

He helped her, and when the last of his clothes was on the floor he said solemnly, 'You can stop now.'

'So you were lying on the bed—like this?'

'Just like this,' he agreed, letting her press him back against the pillows. 'She slipped in quietly through the door and lay beside me.'

'The hussy!'

'Yes, she was a hussy,' he recalled with a reminiscent smile. 'She knew every trick to excite a man, plus a few that I think she invented, and she used them without mercy.'

'Shameless!'

'Totally shameless. That was the best thing about her.'

'What exactly did she do?'

He laughed softly. 'Why don't you experiment a little, and I'll tell you when you get it right?'

She joined in his laughter, and they shared the

joy that welled up in them both, until at last the moment came when she silenced him by laying her mouth over his, sending him a new message, one she'd never felt able to offer before, but which would sustain them for the rest of their lives.

MILLS & BOON PUBLISH EIGHT LARGE PRINT TITLES A MONTH. THESE ARE THE EIGHT TITLES FOR SEPTEMBER 2008.

———————— ∅ ————————

THE MARKONOS BRIDE
Michelle Reid

THE ITALIAN'S PASSIONATE REVENGE
Lucy Gordon

THE GREEK TYCOON'S BABY BARGAIN
Sharon Kendrick

DI CESARE'S PREGNANT MISTRESS
Chantelle Shaw

HIS PREGNANT HOUSEKEEPER
Caroline Anderson

THE ITALIAN PLAYBOY'S SECRET SON
Rebecca Winters

HER SHEIKH BOSS
Carol Grace

WANTED: WHITE WEDDING
Natasha Oakley

 MILLS & BOON®
Pure reading pleasure™

0808 Rom LP

MILLS & BOON PUBLISH EIGHT LARGE PRINT TITLES A MONTH. THESE ARE THE EIGHT TITLES FOR OCTOBER 2008.

—————— ✑ ——————

THE SHEIKH'S BLACKMAILED MISTRESS
Penny Jordan

THE MILLIONAIRE'S INEXPERIENCED LOVE-SLAVE
Miranda Lee

BOUGHT: THE GREEK'S INNOCENT VIRGIN
Sarah Morgan

BEDDED AT THE BILLIONAIRE'S CONVENIENCE
Cathy Williams

THE PREGNANCY PROMISE
Barbara McMahon

THE ITALIAN'S CINDERELLA BRIDE
Lucy Gordon

SAYING YES TO THE MILLIONAIRE
Fiona Harper

HER ROYAL WEDDING WISH
Cara Colter

◉™ MILLS & BOON®
Pure reading pleasure™

0908 Rom LP